Now Sophie would upset him further!

She said, 'You seem to be under a misapprehension. We are not confining ourselves to small-animal work. We are just as interested in large animals — lots of farms round here.'

Obviously startled, the two men stared incredulously. Then Robert said grimly, 'Well, there, I'm afraid, you'll really come unstuck. Farmers don't, on the whole, like women vets to do their work and they don't change easily.'

'Oh, yes, we know that,' Sophie smiled scornfully. 'So it's going to be up to us to show them how mistaken they are.'

Dear Reader

We travel again this month, to Spain and Australia in SWEET DECEIVER by Jenny Ashe, and OUTBACK DOCTOR by Elisabeth Scott. We also welcome back Elizabeth Fulton with CROSSMATCHED where American new broom Matt Dunnegan shakes up renal nurse Catherine, and Mary Bowring, who returns with more of her lovely vet stories in VETS IN OPPOSITION. Just the thing to curl up with by the fire as winter nights draw in! Enjoy.

The Editor

Mary Bowring was born in Suffolk, educated in a convent school in Belgium, and joined the W.A.A.F. during World War II, when she met her husband. She began to write after the birth of her two children, and published three books about her life as a veterinary surgeon's wife before turning to Medical Romances.

Recent titles by the same author:

VETS AT VARIANCE
VET IN CHARGE

VETS IN OPPOSITION

BY
MARY BOWRING

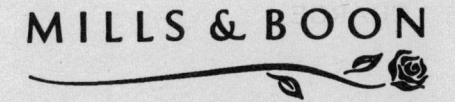

MILLS & BOON

MILLS & BOON LIMITED
ETON HOUSE, 18–24 PARADISE ROAD
RICHMOND, SURREY, TW9 1SR

All the characters in this book have no existence outside the imagination of the Author, and have no relation whatsoever to anyone bearing the same name or names. They are not even distantly inspired by any individual known or unknown to the Author, and all the incidents are pure invention.

All Rights Reserved. The text of this publication or any part thereof may not be reproduced or transmitted in any form or by any means, electronic or mechanical, including photocopying, recording, storage in an information retrieval system, or otherwise, without the written permission of the publisher.

This book is sold subject to the condition that it shall not, by way of trade or otherwise, be lent, resold, hired out or otherwise circulated without the prior consent of the publisher in any form of binding or cover other than that in which it is published and without a similar condition including this condition being imposed on the subsequent purchaser.

*First published in Great Britain 1993
by Mills & Boon Limited*

© Mary Bowring 1993

*Australian copyright 1993
Philippine copyright 1993
This edition 1993*

ISBN 0 263 78375 8

*Set in 10 on 12 pt Linotron Times
03-9311-54227*

*Typeset in Great Britain by Centracet, Cambridge
Made and printed in Great Britain*

CHAPTER ONE

THE lecture ended on a humorous note and, as the laughter and applause died away, Sophie Ferguson rose to her feet and followed her veterinary colleagues towards the door. Most of them seemed to be going in search of tea and for a moment, she hesitated. Should she join the group of young vets who had qualified with her two years ago or should she go straight back to her godmother's house, where she was staying for the duration of this annual veterinary congress? It had been a long day and she had absorbed a lot of information on the subject that was uppermost in her mind. Now she felt the need to be alone for a while in order to look over her notes and see if they would help her in her plans for the future. She shook her head, smiled at the beckoning group, and made her way steadily towards the exit.

Several men turned to watch her progress with open admiration, and this was not surprising for she was very beautiful: tall, slim and graceful with dark, shining hair just touching her shoulders, a lovely skin and a soft, smiling mouth. But it was her eyes that drew most attention. Like brilliant sapphires, they shone vividly under long, dark eyelashes and gently curving eyebrows.

Reaching the main hall at last, she mingled with a crowd emerging from another lecture theatre, and suddenly she drew a quick breath and stopped. Surely that was Joanna Kennedy? That vivid auburn hair was unmistakable, and when a laugh rang out her guess was confirmed.

'Joanna!' She tried to make her voice heard above the general clamour and hurried forward, only to lose sight of her quarry in the crowd. Determinedly, with many excuse me's, she squeezed her way through the doorway and looked around searchingly. Yes — there she was, and this time she turned in response to Sophie's call.

Oblivious to the milling crush around them, they stood staring delightedly at each other.

Joanna spoke first. 'Quick! Let's go and grab a table for tea. I'd no idea you were here.'

'Nor I you,' Sophie said. 'It's great to see you again. I tried to contact you from time to time but you always seemed to be somewhere else.'

'I've been doing locums,' Joanna said briefly. 'Look, there's a table for two over there. Let's get it.'

For half an hour they talked over student days and student friends and then there was a long pause. Sophie sat back and surveyed her friend.

'So what now? Are you going on doing locums?'

Joanna shook her head. 'No. I've had enough. Invaluable experience, of course, but I found it frustrating in that, so often, I wasn't able to see cases right through.' She paused. 'I'm going to try and get a job with a view to eventual partnership.' She shrugged ruefully. 'And "eventual" is the operative word. Partnerships take ages to come up.' She looked curiously at her friend. 'What about you? The last card I had from you, you were working in London. I wouldn't fancy that much. Did the bright lights make up for the lack of country life? Lots of glamorous men, theatres, the night-life et cetera?' She grinned. 'Of course with your looks you'd probably have a marvellous time. How do you manage to look so smashing? You're even slimmer than when we were students. Are you on a perpetual diet like me?'

Sophie laughed. 'It doesn't seem to matter what I eat. I stay much the same. As regards London—yes, I did miss the country. After all, I was brought up there and in the end I began to feel stifled. As for the bright lights—I had very little time to enjoy them. I left a month ago.'

Joanna stared. 'You mean you just packed it in? Have you got another job?'

Sophie hesitated, smiled a little mysteriously, then said slowly. 'No. I'm working on a scheme. Something I've always wanted to do. That's why I came to this veterinary congress. I've listened to all the lectures that were about my plan. I thought I would do it alone, but now I've met you again I've changed it a bit.' She paused. 'How would you like to come in with me? I'm going to set up on my own—put my plate up.'

Joanna blinked several times and sat bolt upright on her chair. 'Good lord! That's fantastic! And me—you'd like me to work for you?'

'No,' said Sophie firmly. 'Not *for* me. *With* me. Equal partners.'

Joanna put up her hand. 'Hold on. Wait a minute. I haven't any capital. Well, nothing to speak of.'

'I'm not asking for capital. I haven't got much myself, though I've been saving hard. We'd have to start from practically nothing. We might be able to borrow a bit from a bank, although I'm not even sure about that. But I'll manage something. I'd made up my mind to go it alone before I came here. I've been attending all the lectures that deal with building up a practice; I've learnt a lot and I'm convinced it's possible.' She paused, her beautiful eyes alight with enthusiasm as she leaned forward. 'Then when I saw you I realised suddenly that you were just the friend who would help to make it all a success. You never minded taking a risk, and, of course, that's what it is. Think, Joanna—Ferguson and Kennedy on the plate outside the surgery. It can be Kennedy and Ferguson if you like—I really don't mind. We'd be equal partners.'

Joanna drew a long breath. 'Ferguson and Kennedy,' she repeated mechanically. 'Your name should come first. It's your idea.' Then she shook her head. 'What am I saying? It's not possible, Sophie. Have you thought it out properly? Premises first of all. We couldn't afford to buy and rents are exorbitant. Then all the equipment needed for the surgery. Modern technology. Drugs, instruments, lots of money to be spent before we have even one client.' She stopped, shook her mane of auburn hair, and added ruefully, 'All I've got is my microscope.'

'Plus two years of good experience—the same as I have,' Sophie said calmly. She sat back and smiled. 'Now listen. First point: premises. I've got them.' She paused. 'I'd better begin at the beginning. As I said, I came to the congress to learn about starting up a practice. I haven't taken the accommodation provided here because my godmother lives in Wakefield, a village only five miles away, so I'm staying with her. She's a widow and lives in a big house with outbuildings, et cetera, which is now too large for her. She was thinking of moving to a smaller place, but it's against all her inclinations. She loves her home and has enough money to stay on, but finds it lonely. She and her husband never had any children. When I told her I was longing to start up on my own she suggested I should take advantage of some of the outhouses—convert them into surgery, waiting-room, office et cetera—and have several rooms in the house for myself. She's kept the upper floor, turned it into a very nice flat for herself, and I—you also if you agree—could live downstairs. She's already obtained planning permission for the outbuildings. The situation is good—at the end of a lovely village. Well, it's growing and it's more like a small town now and—hey! What's the matter? You've gone all shaky. You'll spill that tea if you're not careful.'

Joanna put down her cup and drew a long breath.

'No wonder I'm shaking. I can't believe I'm not dreaming. Talk about a fairy godmother.'

Sophie nodded. 'Yes, she's a lovely person. We've always got on well together. She was my mother's best friend and when my parents. . .' She stopped suddenly and Joanna nodded sympathetically.

'That terrible car crash.'

Sophie swallowed hard, then she drained her cup and glanced at her watch. 'Look. Everybody's leaving. Do you want to go to any more lectures?'

Joanna shook her head. 'No. I've had enough. Enough of the social side as well. I went to the congress banquet last night—very grand. I didn't see you there, though.'

'No, I didn't have a ticket. I haven't really taken a full part in the congress. Just wanted to learn about running a practice.' Sophie laughed. 'I've got a one-track mind at the moment.' She paused, then added diffidently, 'I don't want to rush you into anything, but how about coming back with me? You could have a good look around and, of course, meet my godmother.

Her name is Mrs Langton, but she likes to be called Helen.' She paused. 'Of course, if you'd rather do something else this evening. . .'

Joanna got up from the table. 'Nothing could be more exciting than this. Let's go.'

Leaving the seaside resort behind them, they drove out towards the country and soon they came to Wakefield. Joanna said appreciatively, 'It's lovely. A real picture-postcard village. Are those the Downs over there?'

Sophie nodded. 'Yes, and several small villages are tucked away among them. There's also a large estate of new houses on the other side—all future clients, I hope.'

As she waited at the only traffic lights in the main street, her attention was caught as a man came out from a hardware shop. A tall, broad-shouldered man whose looks seemed to epitomise her dream of the ideal man. There was a curious magnetism about him that, for one brief moment, caused her heart to miss a beat, but a blast on the horn of an impatient motorist behind her brought her quickly back to reality.

'Sorry about that,' she said to Joanna. 'I was dreaming.'

As she passed through the lights she turned right into a small service road which ran alongside a few small shops. In one of the few remaining parking spaces she pulled up.

'Joanna—I shan't be a minute. I just want to look into that antique shop. I've had my eye on something and I'd like to see if it's still there.'

Joanna nodded equably and Sophie got out and walked back a short distance. She stood looking in the window, then gave a little sigh. The Waterford vase had gone—she had missed her opportunity. Shrugging regretfully, she continued to gaze at the various treasures displayed.

'Beautiful, isn't it?' The deep voice behind her made her jump and, turning quickly, she met the smiling face of the man who had attracted her attention a short while back.

'Sorry to startle you.' He grinned apologetically. 'But you were looking so absorbed that I guessed you were admiring that wonderful bureau.' He pointed to the centre of the window. 'It must be worth a fortune. Any idea how old it is?'

Sophie's interest was aroused. 'Well, it's eighteenth-century, I should think. That Dutch floral marquetry is lovely, isn't it?'

His eyes—a brilliant hazel—widened appreciatively. 'So you know your antiques, do you? Meet a fellow enthusiast. Not very knowledgeable as yet, but anxious to learn.' He paused. 'I'm new to this village. Do you live around here?' His mouth twitched at the corner. 'I hope you do.'

Sophie flushed at the open admiration in his eyes.

'Not yet, but I soon will be.' Then, remembering that Joanna was waiting, she added quickly, 'I must go,' and began to move away.

He took a few steps with her. 'Well, perhaps when you are settled here we might get together and tour the local antique shops.'

She hesitated, then said evasively, 'Perhaps. Now I really must go. My friend is waiting.'

As she went towards her car she heard him call, 'I'll look out for you.'

Getting into the driving seat, she laughed at the open curiosity on Joanna's face.

'Nice-looking man,' she said. 'Friend of yours?'

'Never seen him before. We were just both admiring a lovely antique bureau.' For some reason Sophie was reluctant to mention her first sighting of him and the effect it had had on her.

'Well, well. . .' Joanna grinned. 'That's one way of scraping acquaintance. From what I could see in the mirror he looked more interested in you than in the bureau.'

'Idiot!' Sophie laughed, but there was a warm feeling in her heart as she contemplated the fact that in such a small place it was quite likely she would encounter her chance acquaintance again.

A little further on she turned left down a quiet lane and pulled up outside two large gates in the centre of high walls.

'There's the house.' She pointed. 'It's quite old, as you can see.'

It stood four square, its dark red walls half covered with large-leafed Virginia creeper just beginning to change from green to gold and russet colours. The Queen-Anne-style windows shining in the reflected rays of the setting sun and the outbuildings clustered round it gave the impression of a small manor house.

Joanna drew a long breath. 'I'm stunned. It's absolutely lovely, but——' She stopped and shook her head. '—We'll never be able to afford the rent.'

'Well, of course we couldn't if we had to, but my godmother really is a fairy godmother. I told you, she's comfortably off and she wants to help me. She won't take any rent—says the fact that I will be in the house and that the outbuildings will be put to good use is enough. All the same, I insisted that we should pay our share of the electricity, heating, et cetera, and made her agree to that. By the time those bills come in, we should have made enough to cover them. What do you think? Are you willing to live on bread and cheese and baked beans for a while?' She paused and smiled. 'At the moment Helen is cooking enormous meals for me, but I've told her I insist on looking after myself once I start working.' She pulled the ignition key. 'Come on. Meet Helen, see if you like her, and then you can think it over and give me your decision later. If you don't care for the idea I shall understand.'

Joanna said slowly, 'Suppose I turn it down. What will you do? Find someone else to share with you?'

'Oh, no,' Sophie said decisively. 'I wouldn't want anyone else. I planned to do it alone in the first place.'

'But you'd want someone to assist you — a veterinary nurse to help with operations, et cetera.'

'Helen has offered to do anything necessary in that way. She's used to animals. She says she'd love it. Even if you come in with me, I'm sure she'd be very useful. Look — there she is, just coming in from the garden.'

A tall, slim woman in her early fifties waved as the car approached and, walking with a long, easy stride, she came towards them. She had short dark hair, wore well-cut trousers, a green country jacket and long, mud-splashed boots. Two dogs — a Springer spaniel and a black Labrador — followed close at her heels and, as Sophie pulled up, they rushed towards the car. A sharp word of command and they immediately sat down and waited as their mistress opened the car door.

With a few words of explanation Sophie made the introduction and as they walked together into the house her godmother said, 'I'm afraid I've got some news which won't please you, but first of all I want to hear yours.'

Passing through a square, oak-panelled hall, Helen opened a door at the end and turned to Joanna.

'All our discussions take place in the kitchen. I always think of it as the engine-room of the house. There's a meal in the oven so let's have a sherry first, or if you would prefer a soft drink you have only to say.'

Settled round a large pine table with their assorted drinks, Helen listened attentively as Sophie revealed her new plan. Then she nodded thoughtfully.

'It sounds a very good idea, especially in view of what I have to tell you.' She smiled at Joanna. 'You're most welcome here. There's plenty of room, as you can see, and I'm certain that two hands must be better than one in a veterinary practice. Now that brings me to my news, which I hope will not alarm you too much.'

'Oh, dear!' Sophie said. 'Is it something to do with planning permission?'

Helen shook her head. 'No. That's all settled.' She shrugged ruefully. 'I ought to have found this out before, especially as I usually know everything that goes on in this village, but they've managed to keep it secret. It's now a *fait accompli* and a surprise to everyone.'

'What is?' Sophie's voice trembled. 'What on earth are you talking about?'

Helen heaved a sigh, took a sip of sherry, then said slowly, 'At the other end of Wakefield—the far end of the High Street—is the house where old Dr Watson lived. A few months ago he died, and his wife sold the house and went to live with her sister. This morning Betty—my cleaner—came in bursting with the news that there was a brass plate outside. Thinking it meant the arrival of a new doctor, she stopped to read the two names on it. Sophie, my dear, it's a veterinary practice. Two men—R. H. Sheldrake and I. C. Woodall.'

Sophie's face whitened and Joanna sat rigid with shock as Helen continued, 'It's awful, isn't it? I was shaken to the core at first, then Betty—she knows all our plans, of course, and is full of enthusiasm, though she is utterly discreet—she put the situation in perspective. She said, 'What does it matter? Those two men vets will have so much work with the farms around here; there's surely room for a lady vet to do the small animals. That new estate—dogs and cats everywhere.'

'That's all very well,' Sophie said unhappily, 'but we don't want to confine ourselves to household pets, do we, Joanna?'

'Of course not.' Joanna looked equally gloomy. 'We want to do the lot. A mixed practice. Besides, those two men will have surgery hours on their plate, which means small animals as well.'

There was a long silence broken only by the ticking of the grandfather clock and the sighs and movements of the dogs stretched out on the floor. Then, suddenly, humping her shoulders, Sophie said, 'Well, we'll have to do the correct thing and inform them that we're going to set up here. There's nothing they can do about it, you know. We've a perfect right to practise where we like.'

Joanna stared and Helen gave a quiet chuckle.

'Good for you, Sophie. I might have known you wouldn't run away from opposition.'

Joanna said in a high, incredulous voice, 'But surely

you're not going ahead with it? We ought to look for premises elsewhere.'

'I don't see why we should give up these wonderful premises just because there's another practice about a couple of miles away.' Sophie paused and looked reflectively at Joanna's troubled face. 'Look — we've just got to gain people's confidence and prove that we're better and more caring than those two wretched men.' She stopped for a moment, then said suddenly, 'Let's look them up in the veterinary register and see roughly how old they are, judging from the year they qualified.'

'What good will that do?' asked Joanna sceptically.

'Well, we'll see what we're up against and where they come from. I've got the latest register somewhere — I think it's in my room. I'll be back in a minute.'

Helen and Joanna sat in silence for a few moments, then the older woman said, 'Don't you think it's worthwhile going ahead, Joanna?'

'Well, judging from the size of the village, there may well be room for us if we're to be content with small animals only, but I'm afraid we'll never get any farm work. It's hard enough to break down the old prejudices — I know that from experience. Farmers will always choose male vets if they have the option.'

She looked up as Sophie returned, leafing through the pages of the veterinary register.

'Here we are — Sheldrake, Robert. Qualified London six years ago. His last address was in Shropshire. Now for I. Woodall. . .' She turned the pages quickly, ran her finger down a column, and said, 'Ah, Ian Woodall, qualified London the same year as Robert Sheldrake. Last address in Hampshire.' She put the book on the table. 'Well, they've had four more years' experience than we have.'

Joanna frowned. 'I don't remember them as students, but then they were years ahead of us. We were small fry compared with them. But the name Woodall rings a bell. I've got a feeling I've met him somewhere — perhaps on one of my locum jobs.'

Sophie was looking thoughtful. 'Well, now — professional etiquette and all that. The moment we put our plate up, we'll have to go and inform them politely of our presence. That will be a bit tricky — you know, stiff and cold — but we don't have to do it until we're actually here.'

Helen nodded. 'I'll bind Betty over to even more secrecy. Now — how about some food?'

A month later, Sophie and Joanna stood looking round their new domain. Every moment of their spare time had been spent cleaning and painting, and, with the help of Helen's handyman, they had put up shelves and partitions, and the gleaming, spotless rooms did credit to their hard work.

Sophie ticked off items on her fingers. 'Sink with hot and cold water, gas, electricity, telephone with extension to the house, surgery table — that second-hand adjustable table was a real bargain — recovery cages, filing-cabinets, anaesthetic machine, instruments. . .'

'To say nothing of my microscope.' Joanna grinned. 'I reckon we've got the minimum necessary.'

'Later on,' Sophie said, 'we'll get a computer and other technical wonders.'

Joanna said, 'I had an uncle — he's dead now, but I used to spend a lot of time in his surgery — and, apart from the essentials, he never went in for what he called expensive gimmicks. He had a flourishing practice, nevertheless.'

Sophie went to look out of the window. 'It's getting dark now — we'll put our plate up tomorrow, then we'll have to go and break the news to Messrs Sheldrake and Woodall.'

Joanna heaved a nervous sigh. 'I'm not looking forward to that, are you?'

'In a way I am,' Sophie said. 'I dare say they'll hate us, but I don't mind that. On the other hand, they might be reasonable. After all, relations between neighbouring vets can sometimes be quite friendly. They often help each other out when it comes to time off and holidays.'

'We should be so lucky,' Joanna said grimly. 'I'm sure they'll be furious and fight us tooth and nail.'

'Well, we'll fight back. We've as much right to be here as they have. We've got several advantages, too. There's plenty of room for cars in the yard — much better than parking in the village street. Then there's Helen, who knows everybody and is highly respected to say nothing of Betty, who will praise us up to the skies even before we've spayed one cat.' She glanced at her watch. 'Come on. We've promised to have a drink with Helen. She's invited a close friend she wants us to meet. He's the local landowner — those fields at the back of these outbuildings are part of his estate. He owns about eight hundred acres. He lives in a lovely eighteenth-century house about a mile away.' She paused and added thoughtfully, 'It's strange, but although I've stayed down here a lot I've never met him, but perhaps that's because his wife was an invalid and he devoted all his time to her. She died last year, soon after Helen's husband died.'

'Well, now that Helen is a widow and this old friend is a widower. . .' Joanna grinned as Sophie burst out laughing.

'You are the limit, Joanna. An incredible romantic. I shouldn't think Helen would want to get married again. Her husband was a bit of what my mother called "a ladies' man". He even entertained them down here, but she took it all in her stride. She's a tough lady underneath that quiet exterior.'

'Ah, well. . .' Joanna shrugged ruefully. 'Perhaps I am a romantic. With my figure I can only dream. All the same, I've certainly got the right shape for dealing with large animals — look. . .' She held out her right arm. 'I can cope with even the most difficult calving case, as I've already proved to quite a few doubtful farmers.'

Helen's flat looked charming, furnished as it was with choice pieces of antique furniture, their surfaces glowing in the soft light. As the two girls entered, a man rose from a deep armchair, and Sophie looked at him with interest. A tall man of about sixty, he was dressed in expensive country clothes. His thick grey hair was well groomed, his keen eyes looked kind, and his handshake was firm. His name was Edward Greenwood, and as they all sat down, he said, 'I've heard all about you from Helen and I wish you the best of luck. You'll be up against it with those two young men so near you. I've met them — they're very nice, you know. You ought to be on friendly terms. I'm sure this village and the surrounding ones will provide enough work for two veterinary practices. Helen tells me you want to do farm work as well, and although I'm told women vets are just as good as men I've yet to be convinced. I'll try to be neutral. My vet — an older man who lived out on the Downs—has just retired, so I'll try both your practices which will be to my advantage, because when one practice is too busy to come out at once then I can call on the other.'

'Oh, but you can't dice about like that,' Joanna said boldly. 'From the vets' point of view it's not ethical.'

Edward Greenwood raised his eyebrows. 'Maybe not,' he said calmly, 'but I'm not a vet. I expect I'll find a way of testing your different abilities. Of course——' he paused, '—I could ask you to look after my small animals and give the farm work to your colleagues, but I gather that wouldn't suit you at all.' He accepted a glass from Helen and looked at her quizzically. 'You think I should hand all my work to your goddaughter, but I'm not so sure. So I'll test them both out.'

Sophie glanced at Joanna, who shrugged, then at Helen, who was looking anxious, and, although Mr Greenwood's attitude towards professional etiquette was more than a little arrogant, the last thing she wanted to do was to upset her godmother. She said evenly, 'I understand your point of view, Mr Greenwood. However, Joanna and I must be strictly ethical. We wouldn't like to be hauled over the coals by the veterinary council for unprofessional conduct.'

Edward Greenwood nodded thoughtfully. 'Quite right, quite right.' He turned to Helen. 'I was doubtful when you told me about sharing your house with two young vets, but now I think you were right. They're going to liven things up around here. They deserve to succeed.'

He left before they did and Helen said, 'You mustn't mind Edward. He's one of the old school—thinks women need to be protected and all that.'

'Nice,' said Joanna, then grinned as she caught her friend's eye. She added apologetically, 'Sophie thinks I'm too romantic, and I suppose I am, but I must admit I'd love to be protected.'

Helen laughed. 'Well, I think you're going to need protection tomorrow when you go to announce your arrival on the veterinary scene. By the way, I hear from Betty that there is a veterinary nurse there who is a bit of a dragon.' She turned to Sophie. 'Have you made an appointment for tomorrow?'

Sophie nodded. 'I wrote a letter two days ago suggesting a meeting and this morning I got back a curt note suggesting a time. So think of us tomorrow morning at ten-thirty.'

'Come and have coffee with me as soon as you get back,' Helen said. 'I'll be on tenterhooks. I just hope it won't be too unpleasant for you.'

'It shouldn't be. After all, we're in the same profession—caring for the health and welfare of animals. That should come above financial gain.'

'That's the way it should be,' said Joanna, then added grimly, 'but, having been a locum in many practices. . .' She shrugged. 'Well, least said, soonest mended.'

'I expect those two young men will behave as they ought,' said Helen. 'It may not be as bad as you expect.'

It was a bright morning with a hint of autumn in the air when, full of elation, the two girls fixed their well-polished plate on the gatepost and stood back to admire it.

'I think three surgery times are necessary,' said Sophie. 'We shall probably have mostly small animals at first.' She glanced at her watch. 'Nearly time to go. We mustn't be late for our appointment.'

A tall, good-looking blonde veterinary nurse opened the door to them, and her face froze as they announced themselves.

'I'll just see if it's convenient,' she said stiffly and turned away quickly, leaving them on the doorstep.

'Not the most polite reception,' Joanna murmured. 'I think our fame has gone before us, don't you? If she meant to make us nervous, she's succeeded as far as I'm concerned. I'm shaking.'

'You mustn't show it,' Sophie said firmly. 'Remember we're their equals. Don't let them get away with being patronising, because that's probably the attitude they'll take up.'

Ushered in at last, passing through a spotless surgery agleam with modern equipment, and offered seats in an equally efficient-looking office, Sophie's heart jerked suddenly at the sight of the man who was holding out his hand. Tall, broad and muscular, hazel eyes under dark eyebrows, strong features in a tanned face — it was the man in the village street towards whom she had felt such a strange attraction. The shock was mutual, for Sophie saw his eyes widen in astonishment, but his momentary smile of pleasure was instantly suppressed. He said smoothly, 'What a coincidence!' He paused, then added stiffly, 'How do you do? I'm Robert Sheldrake and this is my assistant, Ian Woodall.'

She said calmly. 'I'm Sophie Ferguson and my partner here is Joanna Kennedy. I suppose you can guess why we've come to see you.'

He nodded. 'When I got your letter, I made a few

enquiries and discovered that you are intending to practise from Broom House. Right?'

'Yes,' she said briefly, and for a few moments they studied each other. Sophie's heart sank a little as she saw the grim line of his mouth but his eyes at first showed open admiration as they swept over her. Then almost instantly they hardened and grew hostile. Before she could say anything, however, she was astonished to hear Joanna's attractive chuckle as she turned and indicated Ian Woodall.

'What do you know? Ian and I worked together about a year ago when I did a locum in the practice where he was an assistant.'

The stocky fair-haired young man smiled in friendly fashion, but Robert Sheldrake frowned. He said, 'Well, you may have worked together then, but the situation is quite different now. We look upon you as unwelcome opposition. That is, as far as small animals are concerned. You won't, of course, affect our large-animal work.'

Joanna's mouth opened and Sophie could see that she was on the verge of an angry retort but the situation was saved by the entry of the veterinary nurse, carrying a tray.

'Ah, here's Dawn with coffee.' He waved a hand towards his visitors. 'Meet Miss Ferguson and Miss Kennedy—the two vets who are setting up at Broom House.' He paused. 'This is Dawn Hopwood, our very capable veterinary nurse.' He glanced at the tray. 'No cup for you, Dawn? Don't you want any?'

'No, thank you.' She shook her head. 'I've got things to do in the dispensary.' A cold nod towards Sophie and she went quickly out of the room, leaving behind an uncomfortable silence. At last Robert Sheldrake said, 'Good veterinary nurses are sometimes difficult to find, but Dawn is an old friend who has come to help us out in our new venture.' He handed Sophie a plate of biscuits and as she shook her head he said with a hint of mockery in his voice, 'No? You should, you know. Help to keep up your strength. You'll need plenty in the struggle that lies ahead.'

Sophie felt a surge of anger, but with an effort she suppressed it. She shrugged and glanced at Joanna, who seemed to be getting on well with Ian Woodall. They were reminiscing over the times they had worked together, and this she found irritating. This meeting was not turning out as she had planned. Robert Sheldrake was taking it for granted that the only threat to his practice was that of two small-animal vets, and even that was sufficient for him to be rather unpleasant. Well, now she would upset him further.

She said, 'You seem to be under a misapprehension. We are not confining ourselves to small-animal work. We are just as interested in large animals—there are lots of farms round here.'

Obviously startled, the two men stared incredulously. Then Robert said grimly, 'Well, there, I'm afraid, you'll really come unstuck. If you know anything about this part of the country, you will know that Sussex farmers are very conventional. If you hope to break into that side of veterinary work you'll be disappointed. Farmers don't, on the whole, like women vets to do their work, and they don't change easily.'

'Oh, yes, we know that.' Sophie smiled scornfully. 'So it's going to be up to us to show them how mistaken they are.'

Ian Woodall glanced at his companion and laughed uncomfortably. 'That sounds like a declaration of war.'

Turning to Joanna, he added, 'He's right, you know. You haven't a hope where local farmers are concerned.'

Joanna drew herself up. 'Have you forgotten the farms I went to in the Hampshire practice where I was a locum? You said then that I'd never cope, but the farmers liked me enough to ask me to call again.'

He shrugged. 'That was because you were a bit of a novelty. It would have been a different matter if you had been a permanent assistant in the practice. They would only have had you in as a last resort.'

Joanna gasped indignantly, but before she could protest Sophie rose to her feet.

'Well,' she said coldly. 'Now we know where we stand with regard to each other. I think we'll leave it at that. Thank you for the coffee.'

CHAPTER TWO

IN THE relaxed atmosphere of Helen's flat, Sophie gradually calmed down. Everything was out in the open now and the dream she had had for so long was about to turn into reality. Admittedly she had not envisaged opposition, but she must not let that discourage her. Of course, Joanna might get a bit depressed if very little farm work came along, but maybe Robert Sheldrake's gloomy prediction would prove to be wrong.

Helen's voice broke into her thoughts. 'I think your first client has arrived.' Going to the window, she added, 'Yes—a man. . . Ah! I know him—a Mr Jarvis. He's got two little girls with him—one is his daughter. He's carrying something very odd. It looks like a landing net covered by a cloth.' She turned. 'Quickly— you'd better go down to your surgery.'

Joanna chuckled as they ran down the stairs. 'Don't tell me it's a fish in need of first aid.'

They reached the surgery door at the same time as the strange little group and, as they ushered their client in, he said, 'We were just going to Sheldrake and Woodall when we saw your plate on Broom House gate.' He paused, put the rod on the table, and began to take off the cloth. 'Do you know anything about squirrels?' In answer to Sophie's careful nod, he went on, 'My little girl and her friend found this creature in a corner of my yard. He was trying to climb up a brick wall, but he's got a bad leg. I think he's been shot.

Luckily, the children came to me before trying to catch him, or they might have been bitten.

Even through the thick net, it was plain to see that the squirrel's right hind leg was damaged. A patch of dried blood showed on the top where it lay splayed out, and the sight was so pitiful that one of the children began to cry.

'Stop it, Sally,' the elder one said sharply. 'The vet will put it right.' She turned to Sophie, who was studying her patient, and added, 'You will, won't you?'

'I'll do my best,' Sophie promised, then glanced at Joanna. 'It will have to be anaesthetised. Could you fill a syringe for me? I'll put the needle in through the net.' She turned to Mr Jarvis. 'If you hold the net firmly, my partner here could draw it closely round the squirrel so that it can't struggle.'

The children covered their eyes and turned away as the needle went in, but the squirrel only jerked slightly then lay still. Withdrawing the needle, Sophie said, 'It remains to be seen how he takes the shock. We'll leave him for a minute or two, then I'll test his reflexes.' She added conversationally, 'That landing net of yours was a marvellous way to catch him.'

He grinned. 'Well, fishing is my hobby, but it's the first time I've caught a squirrel. Actually it was lucky the children found me. I'd only just come in from seeing to a sick sow—I'm a pig farmer; Mrs Langton here at Broom House knows me well.' He looked curiously at the two girls. 'I suppose you're part of Mr Sheldrake's practice.'

'Oh, no, we're not,' Sophie said quickly. 'We're quite separate. Mrs Langton is my godmother and she's let us take over these outbuildings.'

He looked round appreciatively. 'A nice job you've

made of them, too.' He laughed. 'So now we've got four vets in the village where we never had one before. I always had to call out Mr Davidson—the vet who lived out on the Downs—but he's gone and retired. I suppose I'll have to go to this Sheldrake man for my pigs.'

There was a moment's silence, then Joanna said, 'Why?'

'Why, miss?' Mr Jarvis looked surprised. 'Well, I don't suppose you lady vets do pig work. Can be difficult and a bit dangerous at times.'

'I've done lots of work for pig farmers,' Joanna said boldly. 'The usual pig diseases, castrating piglets—the lot. What makes you think women can't do that kind of work?'

He scratched his head. 'Well, now, you've got me there. It's just that I've never given the matter much thought. Took it for granted, like.'

There was a moment's silence, then Sophie said, 'The squirrel is ready. Let's get him out.'

Laid on the table, it looked very small and pathetic, and as the children approached the smaller one said accusingly, 'He's dead. You've killed him, miss.'

Sophie looked up from testing her patient's reflexes.

'No. Don't worry. He's just in a deep sleep. Now I suggest you two go and sit quietly over there while I examine him.'

They obeyed reluctantly, while Mr Jarvis stood beside Joanna and watched the proceedings with interest. Having felt carefully the whole length of the injured leg, Sophie looked up.

'It's not very bad. I thought the leg might have been broken, but the cause of the trouble is a shot up here.'

She pointed to the patch of dried blood. 'That's where the bullet went in. Now I must get it out.'

Joanna handed her a probe and, inserting it into the wound, Sophie began searching. At last she said, 'I've found it. Forceps, please, Joanna.'

A minute later, she said, 'Here it is. Have a look at it, Mr Jarvis.'

He took it from the forceps and examined it carefully.

'It's a pellet from an air rifle. I expect some of those boys in the village have probably been shooting vermin. They should be more accurate. It's not right to leave a wounded animal — vermin or not.'

Sophie nodded as she cleaned up the wound, then, after giving an injection of antibiotic, she stood for a moment in thought.

'I don't think it needs stitches. He'd probably tear them out anyway. Some antibiotic powder and a dressing should be enough.'

Suddenly the older of the two little girls said, 'Why is a squirrel called vermin, Dad? They don't do any harm.'

'Ah, well, that's not quite true. They're rodents — like rats, only with bushy tails. And they do a certain amount of harm.'

'But they've got to live, Dad. You can't blame them for their nature.'

Her father gazed at her helplessly, then, as Sophie finished her treatment, she paused before putting the squirrel in a recovery cage. 'You're both right, you know.' She smiled at the little girl. 'It's true that you can't blame an animal for its nature, but it's also true that they do a lot of harm. They also spread disease. Do you know that if a dog licks their urine, it can catch something called leptospirosis, which is very, very dangerous.' The children looked bewildered, but she added consolingly, 'That's why dogs have to have an injection every year that protects them against that horrible disease as well as many others.'

'Oh, goodness!' The child looked at her father accusingly. 'Dad—what about Rufus and Candy? Have they had that injection?'

He reddened slowly. 'Well, they had the first one, of course but——' he shrugged '—time slips by, you know, and I think they're a bit overdue for the next one.'

'They're both three years old, so they're in danger now.' She turned to Sophie. 'Can you do that injection, miss?'

'Yes, of course I can. All the same——' she looked at Mr Jarvis apologetically. '—I'm not "touting for trade" as they call it. I didn't even know you had any dogs.'

Mr Jarvis grinned and, as she picked up the squirrel and took him over to the recovery cage, he followed and stood watching as she settled her patient down.

'No need to be embarrassed. I'll get you to do the dogs—my daughter will see to that. Little tyrant she is.' He turned to Joanna. 'You say you've worked with pigs. How about coming out to my farm and having a look at that sow I mentioned? Her milk supply is failing and the litter is a large one.' He added thoughtfully, 'I was going to call in someone from the other practice, but I don't see why. . .' He stopped, and looked at Joanna searchingly. 'Would you like to look after my pigs, Miss—er. . . ?'

'My name is Joanna Kennedy, and Miss Ferguson is Sophie.' Joanna's face glowed. 'I'd be delighted. I'm very interested in pigs. They're so intelligent and full of character. Individuals every one.'

She had struck the right note. As one enthusiast to another they were soon deep in discussion until the children began to get restless. After arranging for Joanna to visit his sick sow within the hour, Mr Jarvis turned to Sophie.

'Best settle up my debt. What do I owe you?'

She laughed. 'Why, nothing. You were just being humane towards a wild animal. The squirrel isn't your property.' She paused, then as he began to protest she added. 'No. Really. I mean it. Besides, our first patient has brought us luck. Two booster injections for your dogs, and the care of your pigs. To say nothing of the pleasure of meeting you and your daughter and friend.'

When the little party had left the surgery, Sophie said, 'I'll give that squirrel some food as soon as he's ready. Milk first of all, then I think tinned dog food would be OK. We'll set him free as soon as he's fit.' She glanced at her watch. 'That's our first surgery over. Let's go and tell Helen all about it.'

Joanna shook her head. 'Not me. I must go to the pig farm. See you later.'

Helen shared Sophie's jubilation and said, 'I know Mr Jarvis. A very hard-working pig farmer. Not rich — few pig farmers are, he tells me — but he knows a lot of the farming community. A very useful client.' She paused. 'I forgot to tell you earlier, but Betty was in Seabourne yesterday and she came back with news that might be important. She saw a notice in the window of an empty shop and found out that a pet shop is going to open up there shortly. That's interesting, isn't it?'

Sophie nodded dubiously. 'I'm not very keen on pet shops. Some of them have been getting strong criticism lately. Of course, there are some good ones and they must have someone to see that the animals are kept healthy.'

'Well, there you are,' said Helen. 'It might be a good one and if you could get an appointment as their vet it would be another feather in your cap.'

'Hmm.' Sophie looked thoughtful. 'It might be a good idea if I just wander into the shop when it opens, let drop the fact that I'm a vet, and see if the owner is interested.' She laughed. 'A few years ago that would have been very much frowned on, but now it doesn't matter. I suppose it would be the sensible thing to do.'

Helen said, 'You can bet Sheldrake and his assistant will do the same.' She sighed. 'What a pity they've set up here. Betty says they're well liked, too. I wonder. . .' She stopped, got up, and went to the window. 'I heard a car—yes, it's Edward.' She turned as Sophie rose quickly. 'Stay for a while longer and see what he has to say. You can always plead work if you get bored.'

Reluctantly Sophie resumed her seat. She had no wish to intrude on Helen's friendship with her neighbour and, unless Edward had something to tell of interest to veterinary work, she resolved to leave as soon as possible.

Edward seemed pleased to see her, however, and as he accepted Helen's offer of coffee, he said, 'Sophie—you don't mind if I call you that, do you?—I was going to seek you in your surgery. I want you to come and look at a week-old bull calf. My herdsman says there's something wrong with it. It's not growing as it should although it's feeding well and is quite lively. Will you come back with me and give Jack Owen the benefit of your opinion?' He paused and smiled at Helen. 'I really came to see Sophie, but I couldn't resist calling on you first.'

She laughed. 'You knew you'd get the coffee you like best. Well, I'll let you go as soon as you've finished that cup.' She turned to Sophie. 'I'll hold the fort for you and ring you if anything comes up.' She looked at Edward and said casually, 'Joanna has gone to see a sow at Mr Jarvis's farm. Apparently she's a pig enthusiast.'

'Hmm.' Edward looked impressed. 'I know that farm. Jarvis has built it up through sheer hard work. He's not an easy man to please, though. Let's hope Joanna will be up to it.'

Sophie said shortly, 'I'm sure she will,' then relapsed into silence and tried to hide her apprehension as she thought of the task that lay ahead. A sick calf was really more in Joanna's line. It would be disastrous if she — Sophie — failed to solve the problem. She got up and smiled down at Edward. 'I'll just go down to the surgery and pick up my case. I'll follow you in my car when you're ready to leave.'

On arrival at the farm Edward introduced her to the herdsman then went on to his house, promising to come back shortly.

Jack Owen was a sturdy, pleasant-looking man who greeted her in friendly fashion, though there was a hint of embarrassment in his manner. Indicating the calf, he said, 'We're hoping to keep this one for breeding, so we've let it suckle for the normal period. It's feeding quite well, but the strange thing is it's not making any progress.' He stood back so that she could get a better view of the little black and white Friesian standing in the straw beside its mother.

Trying not to show that she was completely at a loss,

Sophie made a careful examination, then, taking out her stethoscope, she gestured to the herdsman to hold the calf steady while she listened to her patient's lungs. Suddenly, just as she was beginning to despair, the calf coughed — a harsh, ugly sound which was quite distinctive. She sighed with relief. Taking off the stethoscope, she turned to the herdsman.

'That's your answer,' she said calmly. 'Cuffing pneumonia. It's a mild type, but if not treated it could suddenly develop into an acute form with increased coughing, loss of appetite, fever and fast breathing.' She paused, then looked searchingly at the hersdman. 'Mr Greenwood said you were puzzled, but surely you've met this before, haven't you?'

Jack Owen flushed. 'Well, yes, miss, I have but Mr Greenwood said. . .' He bit his lip then added conversationally, 'I've never really known why it's called "cuffing" pneumonia.'

'Ah, well, that's because a "cuff" or sheath of lymphocyter forms round the bronchioles.' Sophie felt a glow of satisfaction as she bent down to open her case. It was good to know that all her veterinary training had come to her aid in spite of the fact that she had been working for two years with small animals only. Filling a syringe, she said, 'This antibiotic will deal with the trouble. I'll give another tomorrow and the following day. By then it should be OK.'

As she withdrew the needle she heard a car draw up outside. She smiled to herself. So Edward had come back to see how she had got on. He probably expected to find that the problem had been too much for her. Well, he was going to be surprised. But it was she who was surprised when a man's voice said explosively, 'What the hell are you doing here?'

She swung round, empty syringe still in her hand, and found herself staring at Robert Sheldrake. He was no longer the suave, sardonic man of yesterday, but one whose piercing eyes were ablaze with fury as he strode towards her. Without waiting for an explanation he turned on the herdsman.

'What's the meaning of this? I dropped by to make sure everything was OK after that difficult calving and I find another vet here. What's more——' he turned to glare at Sophie '—you didn't inform me that you had been called in. Have you no regard for professional behaviour?'

Before Sophie, half dazed by his accusation, could open her mouth, the herdsman spoke up.

'It's not Miss Ferguson's fault, sir. She didn't know you had done the calving. I was told to keep mum about it.'

'What do you mean?' Sophie found her voice and said angrily, 'Who told you to say nothing?' She paused. 'Was it Mr Greenwood?'

'Well, yes, miss.' Jack Owen said reluctantly. 'It was his way of testing you out—you know, one practice to deal with the cow and the other to treat the calf. I told him you wouldn't like it if you found out, but he said——'

'He said it didn't matter,' another voice joined in, and Edward himself stood in the doorway. 'I suppose it was a bit unethical, but I did warn you.'

He spoke lightly, amusement in his eyes, but there was no response in the two pairs of eyes that stared back at him stonily. Sophie was the first to control her anger. Ignoring Edward, she turned to Robert Sheldrake.

'I've given the calf an injection for "cuff"

pneumonia.' She held out the bottle for him to read the label. 'This one. To be repeated for two more days.' She bent down to put the bottle back in her case, then stood erect. 'You can sort things out with Mr Greenwood. I shan't be calling again.' As she walked, she said over her shoulder, 'I shall be sending in my account, Mr Greenwood, which I hope you will settle as soon as possible.'

Driving back, she managed to keep her anger in control. Her worry now was to find a way in which to tell Helen. She was still puzzling over the problem when she saw Joanna's car coming towards her. As soon as they pulled up in the courtyard of Broom House, Joanna jumped out and said jubilantly, 'Mr Jarvis has been putting me through my paces with regard to pigs. He's absolutely fanatical about them — full of stories about their characters and sounding me about various treatments. Finally he has decided that I'm just the vet he needs to be responsible for their health.' She paused for breath then raced on. 'He's got about a hundred — all kept in marvellous conditions. Not only are their sties roomy and warm, but they are allowed to forage around in a large orchard. No factory-farming methods for him. You must come over and see everything soon.' She paused again. 'Where have you been?'

Sophie said briefly, 'Come into the surgery and I'll tell you.'

As she unfolded her tale Joanna's face fell. At last she said, 'What bad luck! Utterly embarrassing. Embarrassing for Edward, too. I'll bet he never expected that Robert Sheldrake would turn up while you were there.'

Sophie looked thoughtful. 'I hadn't looked at it like

that. I was just so furious that I swept out in high dudgeon. What's worrying me now is how to tell Helen. She's bound to ask how I got on.'

Joanna frowned. 'She'll have to know. Better get it over before she hears a garbled version from Edward.'

'I just hope she won't think we're trouble-makers,' Sophie said unhappily. 'She's very fond of Edward, you know, in spite of her pretended indifference. I'll have to be very tactful.'

'I'll stay here in the surgery,' said Joanna and added rather gloomily, 'I don't suppose I'll be overworked.'

Sophie's spirits were also low as she made her way up to her godmother's flat, but they soon rose when Helen showed immediate indignation on her behalf.

'What a silly little trick—he certainly owes you an apology and I'll see to it that he makes it.'

'Oh, don't say anything to him.' Sophie looked anxious. 'The last thing I want to do is break up your friendship.'

Helen frowned. 'Well, if that's what you're afraid of, don't worry. I know how to deal with Edward.'

Back in the surgery Sophie found Joanna giving the squirrel some milk and saw to her relief that he had not tried to pull off the dressing. Then, with a quick glance at the time, she said, 'Time to go and have some lunch. I'll do afternoon surgery, so why don't you take a few hours off? Do some shopping—get some food in. I think it's time we began fending for ourselves. Helen, I know, would like to keep cooking massive meals for us, but, well—what do you think?'

'I'm with you entirely. She's very kind, but we ought to stand on our own feet. She's done so much for us already.' Joanna grinned. 'I'll spend as little as possible, and, as for now, a sandwich and coffee is all I need. I'm counting the calories—I must slim down a bit.'

It was with a certain amount of satisfaction that they settled down in their own kitchen and discussed their financial situation. Sophie said, 'We've got enough money to keep ourselves going for about six months. That allows time for clients to settle their accounts.'

'Always supposing we have any accounts to send out.' For a moment Joanna looked depressed, then she sat bolt upright as the telephone rang. 'You answer it,' she said. 'I'll just sit here and pray.'

Sophie laughed as she picked up the instrument, then, after listening for a minute, she said, 'Oh, yes. We'll always come out on calls if necessary, and yes, we certainly attend to budgies.' Reaching out for the message pad, she wrote down an address and replaced the receiver.

She smiled at Joanna. 'That was the matron of an old ladies' home in the next village. They keep four budgies and three cats. She would like one of us to call tomorrow to clip the budgies' claws and give boosters to the cats.' She paused. 'And guess how she heard of us?'

Joanna shrugged and waited.

'Mr Jarvis's mother lives there. He rang her just before lunch and recommended us for their pets. Fantastic! The word is going round, thanks to your expertise with pigs.'

Joanna's depression vanished immediately and she set off to do the shopping in high spirits while Sophie, equally elated, went to the surgery.

The squirrel was sleeping when she entered, but he woke instantly and began making agitated noises, obviously indignant at his captivity. Sophie talked to him gently, then put a little more food and water into his cage. For a few moments she stood watching him as with quick little movements he fed himself, his sharp eyes darting suspiciously from side to side. Satisfied, he withdrew to the far corner of the cage and settled down again.

Sophie gazed at him affectionately. 'Funny little creature,' she said softly. 'I shall be quite sorry when you leave us. You've brought us good luck.'

Smiling to herself, she began to write up his case, then, suddenly, she heard the bell ring at the door of the waiting-room. Reproaching herself for not having unlocked it when she had come in from the main door, she rose quickly and went to open up.

'I'm sorry,' she began to apologise as she turned the lock and pulled back the door, 'I should have —' Then she stopped, speechless, as she stared up at the tall figure of Robert Sheldrake.

CHAPTER THREE

As Sophie stood back to let Robert Sheldrake enter, he smiled, and, in spite of her confusion, she noticed how that smile lit up his face. Once more she saw the attractive man she had noticed in the High Street, and her colour rose as she recalled how she had hoped to meet him some day. Seeing her embarrassment, he said drily, 'It's all right. I haven't come to fight. I just wanted to commiserate with you. That was a nasty little trick Mr Greenwood played on us.' He paused. 'Could we go into your office? I'd like to discuss it privately.'

Recovering herself, Sophie said coolly, 'Well, there's no one here at the moment. Still, if you prefer it.'

Leading the way, she went across the surgery to the opposite door, but once inside she did not invite him to sit down. His eyebrows rose slightly at her scarcely hidden hostility, and there was an awkward pause.

At last he said smoothly, 'After you had made your impressive exit, Mr Greenwood was completely taken aback. The herdsman beat a tactful retreat to the end of the cowshed and then I took the opportunity to say what I thought. When I'd finished he hummed and hawed a bit, but finally admitted he was at fault and promised to apologise to you as well. Then he asked me to do his regular work, but I didn't commit myself. I thought I would discuss it with you first.'

Sophie hesitated then; in view of this strictly correct behaviour she felt rather ashamed of her inhospitable attitude. Sitting down, she indicated the other chair. 'There isn't anything really to discuss. I said I wouldn't be calling again and I meant what I said.'

'Ah, yes.' He looked at her quizzically. 'You meant it then, but, if I refused to do the work, wouldn't you be glad to take it on?'

'No,' she said firmly. 'He'd have to look elsewhere for a vet.'

'That would be pretty silly. No vet trying to build up a practice ought to let pride overcome his or her business sense.'

She flushed at the implied rebuke, but retorted, 'Then why haven't you committed yourself? If you hesitate too long you may lose your chance. Seabourne is only five miles away and there are two veterinary practices there.'

'Completely small-animal,' he said calmly, 'but that isn't important. As you are not interested I shall accept Greenwood's offer tomorrow.' He paused. 'What I really want to discuss with you is a plan for the future of our two practices — yours and mine.'

'Mine and my partner's,' Sophie corrected him firmly.

'Well, yes, but. . .' He hesitated for a moment then added, 'What would you say to merging? No ——' he put up his hand '— don't shake your head; just listen to my proposition. If we combined we would soon have a flourishing practice. With two partners and two assistants — Ian Woodall and your partner, who could be your assistant. Just hear me out,' he said sharply as Sophie rose indignantly to her feet. 'I would undertake to pay Miss Kennedy a generous salary and you could refund any capital she may have put in as your partner. Then, later on, when you have both built up the small-animal side, she could have a share of the profits.' He paused reflectively. 'I should think she would welcome a regular salary instead of her present partnership, which can only yield peanuts at the moment.'

Sophie's eyes flashed. 'No,' she said curtly, then, for good measure, she snapped, 'Absolutely not.'

He stared at her incredulously for a moment, then, as he began to speak, she forestalled him.

'I think you're about to say that I don't understand, but I assure you I do. Only too well. So you offer to pay Joanna's salary, and, of course, that would automatically make you her employer. You would then have the right to organise her work and most certainly you would see to it that she had little or no large-animal work. That and the fact that she was only an assistant would make her discontented and, quite possibly, cause her to resign. I, in my turn, would be confined to small-animal work, and you and Ian Woodall would have all the farm work. That's your plan, isn't it?'

He blinked, obviously startled at her cynical summing-up of his offer. At last he said, 'You've made it look like a rather nasty plot to achieve my own ends.'

'That's just what it is,' Sophie said coldly. 'A carefully thought-out plot to get control of your rival's practice.'

He flushed angrily. 'You're wrong. It's a good plan which would be to our mutual advantage. The best way out of a difficult situation.'

'Situation? What situation?'

He sighed. 'How exasperating you are. There are now four vets in this village, which is ridiculous. The fact that Ian and I arrived first gives us priority, and it was extremely foolish of you to set up in opposition.

Two women whose work is of necessity confined to small-animals. The farmers will be our bread and butter and the small-animals our jam.'

'What nonsense!' Sophie's voice was scornful, but, inwardly, her heart sank. There was truth in his harsh summing-up. Suddenly he rose from his chair, gave a quick look round the office, then went across to the window, where he stood looking down into the courtyard. Turning, he said,

'Undoubtedly you've got very good premises with ample parking space. But from what I saw through there in your surgery you haven't much in the way of up-to-date equipment—only the bare necessity. Mind you, if we weren't here you would probably do very well. As it is, I'm sure you will eventually have to come round to my plan.'

Patronising beast, she thought furiously, and, getting up, she said angrily, 'Now you just listen to me. The fact that you are here in Wakefield is a stimulus—a challenge that will inspire us to fight you tooth and nail. Wakefield is not just a village—it's growing fast and its proximity to Seabourne is an advantage. Lots of work there.'

He smiled cynically. 'No reason to suppose that people will come out five miles to see a vet when they already have two good practices in their own town.'

Once more her heart sank, but she shrugged disdainfully.

'You're wasting your time. Why don't you go back to your own surgery and try to drum up some work?' Then she bit her lip as he laughed.

'You're not exactly overworked yourself, are you?' Then, suddenly he turned his head. 'What's that noise?'

She stared for a moment, heard the indignant squeaking of the captive squirrel, and laughed.

'Oh, that's a squirrel recovering from an air-rifle shot. We're going to set him free in a day or two.'

'May I see?' For a moment animosity was swept away by mutual interest and, as she led him towards the recovery cage, she felt a pang of regret that their relationship could not be friendly. He looked at the wary little animal for a few moments, then he asked, 'Did you get the bullet out under anaesthetic?'

She nodded and he said, 'Good. Mind you, local farmers wouldn't approve.'

'Well?' She looked at him curiously. 'What would you have done?'

He gave a slow smile. 'Just what you have done.'

She flushed, feeling a surge of friendliness towards this seemingly ruthless man who showed unexpected compassion towards a small, helpless creature at the mercy of all who carried guns. The silence was broken as the telephone rang and he said, 'I must go. Think over my proposition. I expect you'll come round to it in the end.'

She waited until she heard the outer door close, then she picked up the receiver. To her surprise she heard Joanna's voice.

'I'm in Seabourne and I've found that the pet shop is already open. Now I'm wondering whether to go in and try to find out whether the owner has already got a vet. The only trouble is that I can't help feeling that you might do the job better. You're more tactful than I am. You could come in tomorrow. What do you think?'

Sophie hesitated. There was no doubt that Joanna was inclined to be rather blunt, but, reminding herself that they were equal partners, she said cheerfully, 'Go on in, look around and do your stuff. Mind you, I expect they're already fixed up with a vet. Still, nothing ventured, nothing gained.' She paused then added quickly, 'If it's a bad pet shop — you know what I mean — then I don't think we ought to have anything to do with it.'

She put the telephone back thoughtfully. Somehow it seemed degrading to seek work this way, but vets no longer had to be anonymous. They were allowed to appear on TV and the barriers to professional publicity had been removed. In some ways it was good, though a lot of the older generation of vets didn't like it much. She was still deep in thought when the sound of a car drew her to the window. Two elderly ladies getting out seemed to be having difficulty in trying to persuade a large dog to do the same. Quickly Sophie picked up the telephone and rang through to the house.

'Helen,' she said urgently. 'There's a large dog being brought in. I think I'll need some help. It looks rather undisciplined.'

'I'll be right with you.' Helen sounded pleased and was as good as her word. She came in by the side-door just as the clients arrived, and, taking Joanna's overall from the peg, she followed Sophie into the waiting-room.

The two ladies, breathless after their struggle with their German shepherd dog, announced themselves as the two Misses Bradshaw.

'We were just passing and we saw your plate on the gate,' said the tall elder one, 'and we thought it might be a good idea to — well, try you out.'

'You see,' put in her sister, 'there's nothing wrong with Bruno, but his toenails are rather long. Is that too small a task for you to do? Or ought we be able to do it ourselves? We've never had a big dog before, but we thought in these violent days it might protect us.'

Sophie smiled. 'I'm sure you wouldn't be able to cut his nails yourselves. Even if you could hold him down you might easily cut too far and hurt him.'

'It's not only being unable to hold him down,' said the elder woman, 'it's a question of discipline. He needs training. He's very disobedient.'

As though to prove her point, Bruno jerked his lead out of her hand, broke free, and proceeded to roam around the surgery. Suddenly he was brought up sharp by Helen's voice. Turning, he looked, and in a second she had hold of his collar. Sophie lowered the table and the two of them hoisted the surprised dog on to it and raised the table to a convenient height. Still wondering whether or not they would be able to control Bruno, Sophie found to her surprise that she had underestimated her godmother's capability. Her commanding voice became soothing and the dog grew docile and still. Holding each massive paw firmly, Sophie clipped the nails to the right length then lowered the table. As the dog jumped down he stood by Helen for a moment wagging his tail while she stroked his beautiful head.

'A lovely animal,' she said, and the sisters nodded in agreement, 'but he ought to be trained.'

Sophie smiled to herself as Helen got into her stride, advising them to take him to obedience classes. They went away thanking her for her help, and promised to come back in a few weeks' time when Bruno's booster injection was due. Congratulating themselves on having gained another client, Sophie and Helen sat down to have some tea, and Sophie was just about to tell of Robert Sheldrake's visit when Joanna arrived.

'The pet shop,' she announced, 'is one of the best I've ever seen. I wandered around but was unable to speak to the owner because, according to a girl who was serving customers, he wouldn't be in till tomorrow. I was just going out when a man came in and asked the same question. He said he was involved in animal work and would look in again in order to discuss something with Mr Miller, the owner. I looked at him closely and I think he's probably a vet. Probably from one of the practices in Seabourne.' She paused, suddenly downcast. 'It doesn't look as though we've got a chance.'

'Oh, don't lose heart,' Helen said briskly. 'One of you should go in early tomorrow and try your luck. That man may not be a vet at all.'

'He could be anybody,' Sophie said consolingly. 'An RSPCA inspector, a supplier of pet food and accessories. . .'

She shrugged and Joanna said, 'Well, you go in, then, tomorrow. I'll do morning surgery. It isn't as though we're overworked.'

Sophie pondered. 'I have to go to the old ladies' home, but I could do that later. All right, I'll go.' She paused. 'Now listen. I must tell you something. Robert Sheldrake called in here with a proposition.'

She watched their reactions as she told them of his suggestion, and saw from Joanna's face that she was very disturbed. After a long silence Joanna said thoughtfully, 'Well, he could be right. It might be in our best interests to amalgamate.'

Sophie looked at her friend in dismay. 'But we can't give up like that. Why, we've scarcely begun, and already we have a few clients. Give it six months at least. Besides, haven't you realised what it would mean to you personally? Robert and Ian would get all the farm work.'

'Oh, I can see that.' Joanna's voice was bitter. 'Typical of this male narrow-mindedness.'

'Well, that's how it is,' Helen said grimly. 'It makes your struggle a little harder, that's all. Now in this area there are lots of farms—some large, very efficiently run, like businesses, and some small, struggling ones who naturally jib at paying large veterinary bills. But they have to call in a vet from time to time, and it's with those farmers that I think you'll have most success, just so long as you keep your charges low.'

'That's right.' Sophie nodded gratefully at her godmother's bracing words. 'Let's undercut the opposition.' She paused then added thoughtfully, 'Not very ethical, perhaps, but there's no law that forbids it.'

'How do you know that Sheldrake won't do that himself?' Joanna was still looking depressed, and Sophie shook her head.

'I'm certain he's far too sure of himself for that. He doesn't consider us as rivals in the large-animal field.'

All the same, Sophie felt uneasy. This talk of money—she disliked it intensely. It seemed so commercial and against all her ideals. Joanna, who was watching her keenly, said suddenly, 'I know what you're thinking, Sophie. It goes against the grain, doesn't it? We imagined ourselves in a cosy little country practice, jogging along comfortably and enjoying our work. Now we appear to be engaged in a business venture with the threat of a take-over.'

There was another gloomy silence, then suddenly Sophie rallied.

'For goodness' sake! Let's pull ourselves together.

We're behaving as though we're already beaten. The real battle hasn't even begun.' She hesitated then said slowly, 'All the same, Joanna, I don't want you to feel that you're wasting your time here. I should be awfully sorry if you decided you ought to get a job elsewhere where you would be sure of a good future, but I wouldn't hold it against you. After all, I almost dragged you into this, and if it's not what you hoped for then I've no right to pin you down.'

For a moment Joanna looked as though she couldn't believe what she was hearing. She turned scarlet and said explosively, 'You silly goof! Do you think I'm trying to back out?' She straightened her shoulders. 'It's my character. I'm either up in the clouds or down in the dumps—you ought to know that by now. Of course I don't want to abandon ship. I'm not a rat and this ship isn't sinking, by any means.'

The air seemed to have been cleared at last and evening surgery raised their spirits even more. A cat suffering from alopecia was given an injection of a cortico steriod and a dog brought in by a near-hysterical owner was found to be only badly bruised. It was given an injection against shock and pain and it was taken away by a rejoicing owner. Two dogs received booster injections and a ferret was given an injection against distemper. It was very satisfactory and the two girls went to Helen's flat to celebrate with a drink and discuss the possibility of doing work for the pet shop in Seabourne. This involved looking up the ailments common to exotic animals in order to be prepared for any searching questions by the proprietor.

Next morning Sophie set off for Seabourne, and, after looking in the pet shop window, she went inside and strolled around. Her deep interest in the more unusual animals caused a tall, fair-haired man to approach her.

'Are you searching for anything in particular?' he asked as she stood by a cage containing some little creatures curled up fast asleep.

She smiled. 'No, I don't want to buy anything, but I'd love to look around if I may.'

'Of course. I own this shop — Jim Miller is my name. Those are nocturnal marsupials — that's why they're fast asleep now.'

Sophie followed him from cage to cage and saw that everything was very hygenic and that the accommodation was roomy and warm. There was nothing with which she could find fault, and eventually she turned to Mr Miller and said, 'You've got a wonderful collection here and I'm full of admiration at the way in which you look after them.'

He gave her a searching look. 'Are you more than just a potential customer? Someone sent from the local council, perhaps?'

'No. Nothing like that. My interest is solely concerned with the health of animals. I'm a veterinary surgeon. I practise in Wakefield — just a few miles away.'

He stiffened. 'A vet. That's funny. I had a bit of an up and down with one of your ilk only about an hour ago.'

'So you've already settled for a vet to look after your animals.' Sophie looked disappointed.

'No.' He shook his head vehemently. 'This one wanted to do my work, but when he started telling me that personally he was against all pet shops and would like to see them closed we didn't exactly see eye to eye. I told him that I had another shop in Westmead which has been approved by the Ministry of Environment and the RSPCA and that this one will be run in the same way. However, he still persisted in his arrogant objections, so I got rid of him. I could never work with a man like that and I told him so. However——' he shrugged '—my vet in Westmead can't be expected to come out so far so I've obviously got to find one for this shop.' He stopped. 'Now, what do you know about exotic animals? Snakes, for instance.'

Sophie smiled and said frankly, 'Not a lot. I know they get mouth rot and I know how to treat it, but I'm not too clued up on their habits. That's what you'd have to teach me.'

He nodded approvingly. 'At last! Someone who admits I might know a little more than they do. Now— Miss—Mrs. . .?'

'Miss Ferguson—Sophie,' she put in smoothly, and he nodded.

'Well, you'd better come up to my office and we'll talk things over.'

An hour later Sophie left the pet shop feeling as though she were walking on air. It had been arranged that she should make a regular weekly visit in order to vaccinate all new puppies, do an inspection of all the animals already there, and be on call for any emergency. From her own questioning she had made sure that Mr Miller bought only the best puppies from reliable breeders and, in turn, she had told him of her own circumstances. Applauding her decision to set up her own practice, he had offered his help by promising to mention her name to anyone who might be interested.

On her way back she was in such a state of euphoria that, in order to collect her thoughts, she pulled into the service road opposite the antique shop and sat for a few minutes.

As she stared unseeingly ahead, her mind went back to that first meeting with Robert, and a pang of regret shot through her. The prospect of an interesting friendship had been destroyed and now they were at daggers drawn. If only. . .but she pulled herself sternly out of such wishful thinking and prepared to continue her journey. She was obliged to wait a few minutes while a Land Rover was being manoeuvred into the empty space beside her and then, with a start, she saw the driver. Immediately she put her hand on the ignition key, but she was too late. Robert waved her down as he leapt out, and she was obliged to wait. He smiled as he came round to her side, and it was impossible to ignore him. Reluctantly she lowered her window and waited for him to speak.

'How about forgetting our professional differences and coming with me for a look round the antiques?' He paused. 'Don't shake your head like that—please come. I could do with your advice. There's a small Regency table I've got my eyes on. Relax, Sophie—don't sulk.'

Stung, she said indignantly, 'I never sulk.'

His mouth twitched at the corner. 'Well, then—prove it. Let's enjoy what we have in common.' He opened her car door and her antagonism gradually faded. It could do no harm to have a temporary truce and it would be churlish to refuse to give the advice he wanted.

The proprietor greeted them pleasantly then left them alone while he attended to a customer who had followed them in.

'There's the table.' Robert pointed. 'What do you

think?' I've already looked it over and can't see anything wrong with it, but I don't trust my own judgement.'

Sophie nodded. 'It's very nice. A Pembroke table, about——' she paused. '—about 1800 or 1810, I should think.'

He searched for the price label. 'You're spot-on. Circa 1810.'

She passed her hand over the surface. 'Nicely faded mahogany. There's a sham drawer this end and——' she moved round—'a real one here.' She pulled it open and looked inside. 'It's not absolutely perfect, but that doesn't matter much. See—replacement brass handles. The original ones were wooden knobs. This was often done.'

He stared. 'How on earth can you tell?'

'Well—look here. Put your finger in the drawer. Feel behind the handle and you'll find a small hole. That's where the original knob was screwed in.' She paused. 'You could probably knock a little off the price for that.'

She looked up and saw admiration in his eyes. 'I see that I know very little. Where did you acquire your knowledge?'

She shrugged. 'I've always been interested in old furniture and I've swotted it up a bit in my spare time.' She paused. 'Are you going to buy this table? It's definitely a very nice piece.'

He nodded. 'On your recommendation—yes. It's a present for my mother. Her sixtieth birthday.' He took out his wallet. 'I'll go and settle right now.'

She smiled. 'Well, don't forget to bargain a little.'

As they went out of the shop he grinned. 'Got it for sixty pounds less, thanks to you.' Holding her car door open, he added, 'Will you take me on as your pupil? Come out with me sometimes and tour the antique shops in this district.' He saw her hesitation and added quickly, 'Please.'

She looked doubtful. It was difficult to refuse, yet she felt suspicious. Could there be an ulterior motive behind his request?

As though he had read her mind he added quietly, 'It's all right. Veterinary affairs would be absolutely banned. And it wouldn't be very often — we're both too busy to take much time off.'

She smiled reluctantly. 'Well, when you put it like that — it might be rather pleasant.'

His face lit up. 'Great. Perhaps next week some time.'

Settling herself in her car, she looked at her watch.

'I must hurry back. I hope your mother will like the table.'

She tried to put him out of her mind while she drove along and had almost succeeded when she pulled up outside the surgery and saw a car standing in the yard. Going in, she met Mr Jarvis with his little girl standing by the squirrel's cage.

'We're going to set him free tomorrow,' the child said gleefully. 'Dad's going to drive out to the woods and we're going to open the cage door and let him out. Isn't that lovely?'

Sophie glanced at Joanna, who smiled back.

'He's pulled the dressing off but the wound is healing nicely. Have a look at him. I think he's fit to go and he's so unhappy that it seems unkind to keep him caged up. He's your patient so it depends on you.'

The little creature was sitting as far back in the cage as he could get, obviously frightened at the attention he was receiving. Quite plainly he hated every moment of his captivity. Sophie looked at him closely then turned.

'Yes,' she said, 'he can go tomorrow.' She smiled at the child. 'I think you've saved his life, because without attention that wound would have turned nasty; he would have been in a lot of pain and eventually died.'

The little girl looked wistful. 'I'd love to keep him as a pet.'

Sophie shook her head. 'He would always be unhappy. A wild creature like that kept in a cage for the rest of his life — oh, that would be cruel. In any case, it's against the law.' She turned to Mr Jarvis. 'It's good of you to take him off our hands. It will save us a journey.'

He laughed grimly. 'I know I'm being over-sentimental, but there it is. I'm not saying I wouldn't ever shoot vermin, though, but I'd make sure they were dead. And foxes — now they're vicious killers. A year ago a male fox got into my hen house and killed the lot. The wretched animal could only carry away one chicken but he bit the heads off all the others in a sheer lust of killing.'

'But foxes are beautiful,' his daughter protested, and her father said sharply, 'What's that got to do with it? Bluebottles are beautiful and so are wasps, but you wouldn't want to save them, would you?'

The little girl dissolved into giggles, and Mr Jarvis, shrugging helplessly, said ruefully, 'See what I'm up against? It'll be "sweet" little fleas next.'

Leading his daughter, he reiterated his promise to come in after morning surgery to pick up the squirrel and return the cage later, and when the door closed Sophie turned to Joanna.

'Quick. Let's have coffee. I must tell you about the pet shop.'

Joanna had cheered up considerably by the time Sophie had finished, and Sophie's spirits were still high as she drove out to visit the old ladies' home. She pulled up outside a large Victorian house, collected her case, and walked smilingly up the steps to the front door.

Once the budgies and the two cats were attended to, she asked the kindly-looking proprietor if she could have a word with Mrs Jarvis. Over a cup of tea she regaled the old lady with the story of her son and grandchild saving the wounded squirrel, and, leaving her to pass it on to her companions, she drove back to the surgery.

After lunch Joanna asked what kind of progress Sophie thought they were making with small animals.

Sophie grinned. 'Things are looking up. Several dogs have been in for boosters and there's a bitch to be spayed tomorrow. We'll do it together if you're free, and get Helen in as well so that she can learn what goes on. I've also had to put an old cat to sleep, and some children from the new estate brought their hamster in. They thought it was dying from old age, but I didn't think so, though, to tell the truth, I wasn't quite sure what was wrong with it. Then they told me that its companion had just died—it was older—so I rather think it was depressed and lonely. Anyhow I gave them some antibiotic powder to put in its drinking water just in case it had a mild infection and they went away happy and said they would tell their friends.' She laughed. 'I only charged them fifty pence so we won't get rich on that, but it's probably done our reputation a lot of good.' She paused. 'It's beginning to get exciting, isn't it?'

Joanna nodded. 'By the way, Helen wants us to have tea with her. She says she's made a special cake and wants us to help eat it up.'

It was when they were in the process of doing just that that Edward Greenwood walked in unannounced. Helen shook her head in denial as she met Sophie's accusing glance and said, 'Well, this is a pleasant surprise, Edward. What brings you here?'

'I checked with Betty this morning as to whether you'd be in and she said you were making one of your special cakes, so I guessed you would ask the girls up to tea. That's the reason I'm here. I want to apologise to Sophie.'

His look as he glanced across at her resembled so much that of a shamefaced small boy that she found it hard to control a smile. He was obviously not in the habit of apologising, and his rather florid complexion grew even more flushed. He said, 'I ought not to have tricked you like that. Am I forgiven?'

It was impossible to remain resentful in the face of such a frank admission of guilt, and, although her voice sounded rather cool, she said, 'Yes. Of course. I won't think about it any more.'

The slight tension in the room disappeared and she was just going to make some conversational remark when he leaned forward in his chair and said, 'Well, to show that you mean it, will you accept a small invitation? I'm having a few friends in on Saturday evening, along with some new acquaintances, and I'd like you all to come.' He paused. 'Now don't say you can't manage it. You can come when you like after your evening surgery.' He turned to Helen. 'You'll come a little earlier, won't you? I'd like you to act as my hostess, if you wouldn't mind?'

Sophie watched with amusement as Helen's colour rose. She shook her head gently. 'Not as your hostess, Edward. I don't think I want to do that, but I'll come earlier and give a hand — that's if your housekeeper has no objection.'

'You know Mrs Baxter likes you, so don't make excuses,' he said, then added hastily, 'Well, you must do as you like, but I do hope you will come. I think it's time you and I came back into the world. We've both been rather like hermits since. . .' He left the rest of the phrase unfinished, rose from his chair, and added, 'I know my way out, just as I know my way in.'

As soon as the door closed behind him, Joanna burst out, 'That's just what we need — a bit of social life. I love parties.' She turned to Helen. 'Do we dress up?'

Helen smiled. 'Yes, we do rather. Living in the country, we tend to put on a bit of a show on special occasions, and Edward's parties used to be very sought-after. So dig out your prettiest dress.'

As they went downstairs, Joanna said, 'I've got one dress which I wore to the veterinary congress banquet. I suppose I'd better wear that. Otherwise my party clothes are a bit extreme — like me. What about you?'

Sophie looked thoughtful. 'As I told you, I didn't go out much when I worked in London, but I've got a silk dress which I wore on the few times I went to the opera. That will do, I think.' She frowned, then added slowly, 'Joanna do you think Robert and Ian will be there?'

'Oh, lord! I hadn't thought of that. They're almost sure to be, aren't they?'

'I suppose so.' Sophie's frown grew deeper. 'That

puts me right off. I've a good mind to give it a miss. You go, Joanna — you know Ian Woodall, so that won't be embarrassing for you, but I'm blowed if I want to meet Robert Sheldrake socially.'

'Come off it,' Joanna said scathingly. 'Of course you must go. You can't take up that sort of attitude in a small place like this. Are you afraid of him or what?'

'Of course I'm not,' Sophie said indignantly. 'It's just that. . .' She stopped, looking puzzled. 'Well, he rubs me up the wrong way. Ian is OK — friendly and cheerful — but there's something about Robert that makes me want to fight him all the time.'

Joanna looked at her friend curiously for a moment. Then she said bracingly, 'Well, you'll just have to avoid him as much as possible, but you really must go. With only me to represent the practice —— ' she shrugged. ' — it will make us look rather small fry.'

Sophie pondered. Joanna was right. There would undoubtedly be some people at the party who would be intrigued by the arrival of two veterinary practices in their area. She knew from experience how, when anyone heard you were a vet, they immediately began discussing their own pets and their various problems. She and Joanna needed all the publicity possible. She must look on Edward's party as an opportunity not to be missed.

She nodded. 'Yes, I see. Of course I must go. Thanks for putting me straight. Let's go and look out for our glad rags.'

Joanna's emerald-green dress was perfect with her auburn hair and, as she held it up against her, she said, 'I think I'll slit it up the side. Quite a long way, in fact. That will make a few of the men stare.'

Sophie burst out laughing. 'And more likely their

wives frown. Look — I'll slip my dress on and you can tell me if you think it's appropriate for a country gathering.'

She slipped it on. It was so beautifully cut that Joanna gasped in admiration.

'That wonderful royal blue — it emphasises the brilliant blue of your eyes, and you look as slim as a needle. You'll have the men round you like bees round a honey pot.'

Next morning Mr Jarvis rang to tell them of the pleasure he and his daughter with her little friend had had when releasing the squirrel.

'When we put the cage down on the grass and opened the door we thought we might have to urge him out, but not a bit of it. He came out like a rocket and was up a tree before we had time to say goodbye.' He paused. 'Now for something a bit more mundane. One of my sows has a litter about three days old. I spoke to Miss Kennedy about it when she was over here, so would she come now and castrate the male piglets, please?'

Joanna took over the telephone, said she would come immediately, then, putting the instrument back, she grinned at the expression on Sophie's face, then burst out laughing when her friend said, 'Rather you than me. I saw it done once, and the furious sow chased the vet up on to the rafters.'

Joanna shrugged lightly. 'Don't worry, Mr Jarvis has got a huge man to help him deal with that problem. They're going to get the sow into another sty and this man will stand by and see that she doesn't get out to attack us. As for castrating the piglets, it's done in a second and they're passed over to their mother without a clue that their whole lifestyle has been changed.'

Still laughing, she set off, and Sophie settled down to morning surgery. Apart from the cat she was going to spay, no other clients came in, but there was a telephone call from someone who wanted to know how much she charged for a booster injection. When she quoted a figure that was lower than usual the caller immediately fixed an appointment. Replacing the receiver, Sophie smiled triumphantly at the realisation that she must have undercut Robert Sheldrake's fees.

When Helen came in to help with the spaying operation she looked rather nervous. Eyeing the anaesthetic machine, she said, 'Are you sure I'll be able to cope? I'd hate to ruin your reputation by killing your patient.'

Sophie laughed. 'No need to worry. It's perfectly straightforward. Let me show you how it works. You can't go wrong, because I'm so used to doing these operations that I can keep an eye on the cat's breathing at the same time.'

She was just putting in the final sutures when Joanna returned, looking triumphant. Tactfully she waited quietly as she noticed Helen's tension, and as Sophie cut the last thread, covered the wound with antibiotic powder, and bandaged it up, Helen heaved a great sigh of relief.

'My goodness! I was terrified in spite of all your careful instructions. I thought every breath that cat took was going to be her last.'

The two girls laughed and Sophie said, 'You did very well. You were a great help to me. You've got the makings of a good veterinary nurse—that's if you're interested.'

'I'm absolutely enthralled. It's given me a new interest in life. If it doesn't bother you, I'd like to come and watch when you and Joanna operate together.'

Sophie turned to her friend. 'How did you get on with the piglets?'

Joanna's face beamed. 'Most efficiently — Mr Jarvis's own words. There was one awkward moment. The sow was very angry when we took her little boys away and tried to clamber over the wall of the sty. I caught a glimpse of her, eyes red with fury, and I wondered if my last hour had come, but Bill, the man who was on guard, managed to push her back with the aid of a large plank, and she soon quietened down when we passed her babies back.'

Helen shook her head in wonderment. 'The things you girls do nowadays. You say I could make a veterinary nurse — that's as maybe, but I'm sure I'd never be any good as a vet.'

'Well, I thought that once or twice during my years of training,' Sophie admitted, and Joanna agreed.

'It's not anything like as easy as one imagines at the beginning,' she said, 'and when you've actually qualified it's quite frightening when you're confronted by an animal with some mysterious disease and an anxious client standing by. There's not much romance about it then.' She laughed. 'Talking of romance — I passed Robert Sheldrake on my way to the pig farm, and guess who was in the car with him? The glamorous Dawn — his veterinary nurse. He waved to me, but she gave me a menacing glare. Do you think their so-called friendship is more than — well — professional?'

'I hope not,' Sophie said involuntarily, then flushed as she met the others' surprised looks. 'Well, think,' she added quickly, 'think what it would mean. Dawn seems hostile enough already, but if she were to marry him she would take a proprietorial interest in his practice. She might do us a lot of harm. It would be like having three people against us instead of two.'

Joanna grinned wickedly. 'I've got a good idea. A very romantic one. You must get to work and cut her out, Sophie. With your looks, I'm sure it wouldn't be difficult.'

Helen looked amused and Sophie laughed derisively, but, suddenly, she felt as though Joanna had touched on a raw nerve. She said as lightly as she could, 'Nothing romantic in such a calculated scheme.'

'Great fun, though.' Joanna was unrepentant, then she added thoughtfully, 'I wonder if Dawn will be at the party.' She turned to Helen. 'What do you think?'

'I haven't the faintest idea.' Helen paused. 'I wouldn't have thought so, unless Robert Sheldrake has asked if he might bring her with him.'

Somehow the idea depressed Sophie, and although she told herself firmly not to be foolish the party held even less attraction for her. It was just something that must be endured.

CHAPTER FOUR

OVER coffee at the end of morning surgery, Sophie, Joanna and Helen discussed the progress made during the week. Sophie said, 'The word seems to have gone round faster than I would have thought possible. I've had quite a few patients. The usual complaints—eczema, cat bites, chills et cetera, and several booster injections. What's more, the clients are so friendly.'

Joanna grinned. 'I can't say as much for the few farmers I've met—always with the exception of Mr Jarvis, of course. There was that one I went to directly after breakfast this morning. Mr Jarvis had recommended me, but he was very suspicious at first. He told me there was a fifteen-per-cent reduction in milk yield from his herd of cows and wanted to know why. He looked very doubtful when I asked certain questions and laughed me to scorn when I gave my verdict. He said I was just covering up for the fact that I hadn't the faintest idea of what was wrong.'

'Oh, dear.' Helen frowned. 'What *was* your verdict?'

Joanna took a gulp of coffee and grinned. 'Stress—they were suffering from stress. They had just been moved into a new milking shed and they were in completely strange surroundings. What was more, they've had to put up with a relief milker while their herdsman was laid up with flu. "New-fangled" ideas, the farmer said, but I convinced him in the end. You see——' Joanna got into her stride—animals, particularly domestic ones, have thoughts and emotions like us. . . Far dimmer and simpler than ours, but they certainly exist, and it is now recognised that they can and do suffer from stress. Apparently the herdsman is coming back tomorrow, and he's probably gentler with them than the relief milker, and when the cows get used to their new surroundings the milk yield will return to normal. There was nothing else wrong with the herd.' She laughed grimly. 'The best of it was that the farmer — Mr Harris — said that if I proved to be right, he'd call me in again, especially as Mr Jarvis had said that my fees were moderate. Then he had the nerve to suggest that my visit this morning wouldn't cost anything. When I reminded him that I had given expert advice and spent time and petrol on his call, he agreed reluctantly that I had a case. Then he added that times were hard for small farmers and told me not to be in a hurry to send in the account.' She laughed ruefully. 'It seems to me that this practice will only pay its way because of what they now call "companion animals". Any real profit will come from the small animal side.' She sighed. 'If only we could get taken on by three or four large farms with big dairy herds, it would make a tremendous difference — large cheques paid regularly and on time.'

Sophie smiled. 'You know very well that farmers rarely pay on time. They ignore the fact that we vets have to pay our drug bills promptly. I begin to think, though, that Robert Sheldrake was right when he said that the farm work — and in their case they'll probably get plenty — would be their bread and butter, and the small animals their jam. As for us, it will probably be the reverse.' She paused and added wistfully, 'If only. . .'

'Yes, if only Robert and Ian weren't so near,' Joanna

put in. 'Well, it's no use moaning. At least I've got a little farm work.'

'I think we've done jolly well in such a short time,' Sophie said bracingly and added hopefully, 'Perhaps we'll make some new contacts at the party tonight,' and watched thankfully as Joanna's face brightened.

Privately she had her doubts about the party. It would most probably be very staid. Edward's friends would be mostly about his age and fixed in their ways. She rather dreaded the prospect, in spite of the fact that Helen prophesied an enjoyable evening.

No patients turned up for evening surgery, but, for once, that was not depressing. With plenty of time to get ready, Sophie and Joanna were looking their best when they drove to Edward's palatial house. Helen had gone earlier, and when they arrived the number of cars already there made it quite a problem to find a parking space.

The house was ablaze with lights, and the sound of music coming from inside seemed to promise that the party would not be as dull as Sophie feared. Edward looked delighted to see them and, after supplying them with drinks, he introduced them to several other guests. Then he said, 'I've managed to get a sprinkling of young men, and there's one in particular I'd like you to meet.'

He beckoned to a tall, good-looking, fair-haired man in his late twenties, who was talking to Helen.

'My nephew, Giles Brandon. He's spending a week with me and is very interested in what I've told him about you two.'

He disappeared and Giles Brandon stared hard at Sophie.

'We've met before, I think. Perhaps you don't

remember, but you were staying with Helen the year before you qualified as a vet.'

They stood talking and Joanna soon drifted away to a group near by. After a few polite words, Sophie was about to do the same when Giles said, 'Don't go. I'd like to get better acquainted. You've changed a lot since I met you those years ago. You were pretty then, but now——' he stood back and surveyed her so admiringly that it was impossible to take offence '—now you're absolutely beautiful.' He smiled as Sophie flushed and he added, 'I was beginning to wonder if I wouldn't be a bit bored with just my uncle—nice man though he is—but now I'm extremely glad I accepted his invitation.'

This was all quite unexpected and rather exhilarating, and Sophie's interest in Giles began to grow. He was, she learned, a stockbroker in London and, as he quickly informed her, not married. Occasionally he came down to stay with his uncle in order to get a breath of fresh Sussex air.

'Now that I've met you again,' he said meaningly, 'I shall be coming down much more often. The country has suddenly become very attractive.'

Sophie laughed. This pleasant, open admiration was doing wonders for her self-confidence, and once more they plunged into conversation to the exclusion of all around them.

Then, suddenly, from behind Giles, she saw three people come through the door, and her expression froze. Robert, Ian and—yes, that heavily made-up blonde was Dawn.

She averted her gaze and saw that Giles was looking at her in concern.

'I say, I'm not boring you, am I?'

'Of course not.' Apologetically she added, 'Someone I don't like much has just come in, that's all.'

Satisfied, he went on talking, but now Sophie's interest had faded. From the corner of her eye she saw Ian Woodall make a bee-line for Joanna, and they greeted each other with evident pleasure. She frowned involuntarily. It was to be hoped that Joanna didn't let out details of their various clients and the pet shop.

Seeing her frown, Giles turned to look behind him.

'Ah, I get it. That's Robert Sheldrake — the vet who came to my uncle's farm this morning. I was down there looking round and the herdsman introduced us. No wonder you don't like him. I understand he's the opposition to your practice. He looks a tough customer to deal with. He was rather rude to you, I understand.'

'Well, no. Not exactly rude.' Unexpectedly, Sophie found herself defending Robert. 'He has suggested, though, that the two practices should merge, and seemed amazed when I turned down the idea. Joanna and I don't want to be taken over.'

Giles looked thoughtful. 'I should have given it consideration in such a small place as Wakefield. . . It's obvious that the men will get the majority of the work. Farms and all that.'

'I can see that your uncle has been talking to you about us,' Sophie said drily, 'but you don't understand. My godmother — Helen — has given us such good premises and so many other advantages that it would be foolish to give in just because we have a bit of opposition.'

He nodded. 'Yes, I see that. You must have been very angry when Sheldrake got in first — no wonder you hate him.'

'To be fair, I don't hate him. I just resent him

patronising us.' She shrugged and turned away. 'I think we ought to circulate a bit, don't you?'

'I'd rather stay talking to you.' He smiled. 'But you're probably right.'

Suddenly a voice from behind them said silkily, 'How nice to see you again, Miss Ferguson.' Dawn stood beside them, smiling with apparent friendliness. 'Won't you introduce me to your friend?'

Reluctantly Sophie did so, and Dawn's green eyes lit up.

'Mr Greenwood's nephew. How interesting. Have you met Robert Sheldrake—your uncle's vet? He's here somewhere. A brilliant man. I'm his veterinary nurse. Not an easy job, but he's kind enough to say I'm invaluable.'

'I'm sure you must be,' Giles said politely, and, turning to Sophie, who was on the point of moving on, he asked, obviously wanting to detain her, 'Have you got a veterinary nurse?'

It was an unfortunate question and Dawn seized on it before Sophie could answer.

'Oh, Miss Ferguson and her partner only have a very small practice—just companion animals. I don't suppose. . .' She glanced at Sophie maliciously, 'I don't suppose you are busy enough to justify employing a nurse, are you?'

Sophie was speechless for a moment, then, just before she could think of an appropriate retort, Dawn gave Giles a brilliant smile and sauntered off.

'Phew!' Giles drew a long breath. 'That was nasty.' He looked cautiously round the room. 'Do you think she's going about denigrating your practice to all and sundry?'

Sophie felt a chill run through her. Slowly she said,

'It's possible. Look—I'll go and have a word with Robert.'

Picking her way through the guests, she eventually found him talking to Edward, but when he saw her approaching he left his host and came to meet her. She spoke softly in order not to be overheard, but her anger was evident. She asked bluntly, 'Did you put Dawn up to it or is she acting on her own initiative?'

'What on earth. . .?' He looked bewildered. 'What are you talking about?'

She drew a long breath. 'I was talking with Giles Brandon and Dawn came and asked to be introduced. She then made a most offensive and denigrating remark about my practice, and is probably doing the same thing to everyone else here.' She paused. 'I should appreciate it if you would have a few words with her, unless, of course, you approve of such behaviour. In which case, I shall begin making snide remarks about your practice.'

He flushed angrily. 'What exactly did she say?'

She told him word for word, adding coldly, 'Is that how you describe us to anyone who comments on our practice?'

'Of course not. What do you think I am? I can only attribute Dawn's remarks to her excessive loyalty. I apologise for her and I'll put a stop to it.'

'Well, do it now, please, before she does us any more harm.'

'I don't think that's necessary. I'd rather talk to her alone.' He began to move away, but she followed him and he turned. 'Please don't come. I assure you I'll tell her, but I don't want to humiliate her.'

'Well, I do.' Sophie's temper was up. 'She humiliated me quite unnecessarily and I expect an apology.'

He looked at her, his eyes hard and unsmiling. 'You expect too much. Admittedly Dawn has been too outspoken, and she'll have to be told to keep her feelings to herself, just as I do. I suggest you go back to him.' He pointed to the end of the room, where Giles stood looking rather disconsolate. 'Perhaps he'll be able to calm you down. He's obviously struck on you.'

Sophie glared at him. 'Giles sees things clearly, which is more than you do. I suppose you're so besotted with Dawn that you're afraid to tell her off.'

'What? Oh, that's rich!' He burst out laughing, then stopped suddenly. 'I'm not going to bandy words with you. This stupid rivalry has got to come to an end.' He began to walk away, then, once more, he turned. 'Why can't you be like your partner? She and Ian manage to keep their professional lives in proper perspective.'

Involuntarily her eyes followed his and she saw Ian and Joanna talking to friends. His arm was round Joanna's waist and her face was glowing with laughter. Or was it, Sophie wondered, the glow of happiness? She said swiftly, 'That's different. They're old friends.'

'Soon to be more than just friends, I think,' he said sardonically and laughed again as he moved off. This time Sophie made no attempt to follow him. She felt humiliated and depressed and the fact that Joanna and Ian seemed so close did nothing to lift her spirits. Keeping her eyes on Robert as he began to talk to Dawn, she waited to see a change of expression on Dawn's face, then, suddenly, her view was blotted out by a tall figure handing her a glass of wine.

'I thought you might need this,' Giles said drily, and, as she sipped gratefully, he said, 'Listen to that music.

Do you realise that there is dancing in the next room? Nice smoochy music—how about it?'

It was indeed restful and relaxing. Giles was a pleasant companion, but even so the thought of Robert's scorn lingered at the back of her mind. His attitude was more than just mockery. It seemed to embody a deep dislike, and she found that wounding. It hurt her because the feeling he aroused in her was so hard to analyse. He made her angry, but subconsciously she would have liked his approval, would have liked to be on the same terms with him as Joanna was with Ian. Then, remembering how Ian had his arm round Joanna, she saw where her thoughts were leading and shook her head hastily.

Giles looked down at her with a rueful smile.

'What's wrong? Doesn't this kind of dancing meet with your approval?'

Laughing, she managed to reassure him, and when the dance was over, he said, 'Come outside for a while. It's very hot in here and there's a nice balcony through that long window.'

Standing side by side, looking out over the gardens twinkling with lights, Sophie wondered why she felt remote from any romantic interest in her companion. He was talking about his uncle and gradually she realised that his words were meant to impress her.

'Actually, as he and my aunt never had any children, I expect to be his heir.'

She turned to look at him and, even in the dim light, she saw that he was gazing at her meaningly. Chilled, she said drily, 'Well, aren't you lucky? That large estate and this beautiful house—all to be yours one day. You'll have to be careful when it comes to choosing a wife. Make sure she's not marrying you for your money.'

He glanced at her, quickly, recognising the distaste in her voice. He coughed nervously.

'Well, shall we go back and dance a bit more?'

Just as they went inside, she caught a glimpse of Robert and Dawn in an alcove by the door. It only needed a quick glance to see that he had been rebuking her, for her face was flushed and angry and he wore the grim look that made him appear so formidable. As Sophie and Giles came through the doorway, Robert turned quickly away, leaving Dawn alone. Her angry look vanished, and quickly pulling herself together, she smiled at Giles and said, 'I've been trying to persuade Robert to dance with me but without success. He says he wants a word with you, Sophie.' She paused. 'You're going to be left in the lurch, Giles. How about giving me a dance?'

Giles glanced at Sophie and laughed ruefully.

'Well, that's an invitation I can't refuse. See you later, Sophie.'

She watched them go off together, then went in search of Robert, though she found it hard to believe that he really wanted to talk to her. It was, she felt sure, a ploy on Dawn's part, but it left her indifferent. Giles's motive in telling her of his expectations was so transparent that she had lost interest in him. Glancing at her watch, she wondered if she could slip away soon without giving offence to Edward and Helen. Then, as she passed the door of the room where the dancing was, Robert appeared, and there was nothing for it but to repeat Dawn's message.

'Talk with you?' His eyebrows rose. 'Where did she get that idea?'

Sophie shrugged. 'I had my doubts, too,' she said scornfully.

He looked at her searchingly. 'Ah, I see. Giles is the attraction. She wanted to dance with him.' Suddenly he smiled. 'Well, it's not a bad idea, is it? Shall we do the same? Will you bury the hatchet for a while and dance with me?' He saw her hesitation and added softly, 'Please?'

Reluctantly she assented, but her heart was beating fast as he put his arm round her. There was something about this man that set her pulses racing. If only. . .

As though he had read her thoughts, he said quietly, 'We dance well together. What a pity we can't be friends.'

Startled, she looked up at him, met his eyes, and saw in them a searching expression that made her heart jerk in astonishment.

'Come out on to the balcony,' he said. 'We can talk better there.'

Once more she stood gazing out over the garden, but this time everything seemed different—so different that when he took her gently into his arms it was so natural that she made no attempt to draw back. Then his lips came down on hers and she knew this was what she wanted. For a long minute they seemed as one, then, abruptly, the spell was broken.

From behind them came an angry gasp and, as Robert quickly released her, Sophie saw Dawn, her green eyes blazing with fury.

'Robert! How could you?' The words came through clenched teeth, and, lifting her hand, Dawn hit Robert hard on his cheek.

There was a dreadful silence, then Robert said, in a

voice that seemed drained of emotion, 'Dawn—go away. Just go away. I'm not accountable to you.'

She glared at him, then she turned to Sophie.

'He's just using you. He wants your practice and he'll do anything to get it.' Her voice was needle-sharp and her words pierced Sophie's heart.

Robert said sharply, 'That's not true. . .' But it was too late. Dawn disappeared and Sophie was so chilled that she shivered involuntarily. Robert took her arm. 'You're cold. Let's go in.'

She shook him off. 'Don't touch me. Leave me alone. I'm going home.'

As she threaded her way through the guests she forced her lips to smile, though they still felt the pressure of the kiss to which she had yielded so weakly. Dawn's words echoed in her ears, and for all their vindictiveness she knew they must be true. Robert was playing a deep game. If he couldn't get her practice one way, then he would try to get it by another method. And why was Dawn so shocked? Probably because even she had not expected him to sink so low. Bleakly she wondered what the relationship was between them. Had he used Dawn as well? Persuaded her to work for him with promises he had no intention of fulfilling? Suddenly, as Sophie pulled into the drive of Broom House, her pent-up feelings collapsed into cold black depression. When at last she got into bed she allowed herself a few angry tears, then brushed them furiously away. Now that she knew how despicable Robert Sheldrake was, she would fight him with every method at her disposal.

CHAPTER FIVE

NEXT morning at breakfast Joanna seemed not to notice Sophie's depression. As she made coffee she stared dreamily ahead, smiled to herself for no apparent reason, and was so far away that at last Sophie remarked, 'You're very happy—very preoccupied. Is it anything to do with Ian Woodall?'

A piece of toast halfway to her mouth, Joanna nodded then, taking a large bite, she murmured, 'Uhmm.'

Sophie looked apprehensive. 'Well—tell me.'

Reaching for another piece of toast, Joanna said simply, 'We're in love with each other. I'm up in the clouds.'

'Well, it hasn't affected your appetite,' Sophie said tartly, and Joanna laughed.

'It's the other way round with me. When I'm happy I eat, when I'm sad I can't swallow a crumb.' She paused then added more seriously, 'Actually I ought not to be so excited. I ought to be worried. In fact, I am.'

'Worried? How do you mean?'

'It's obvious, isn't it?' Joanna frowned. 'Here we are at loggerheads with the rival practice, and I've gone and fallen in love with Robert's assistant and he with me. He says it'll sort itself out, but I'm not so sure. I can see enormous difficulties ahead.'

So could Sophie, but, not wanting to cast a shadow

on Joanna's happiness, she spoke carefully. 'What does he mean by the situation sorting itself out?'

For a moment Joanna looked troubled.

'He would like us to get married, but I've said that would make things very awkward for you. He sees that too, but the only other option for the moment is that we should. . .' She stopped, shrugged her shoulders, and laughed. 'Well—you know.'

'Become lovers? You needn't be so coy.'

'Lovers, yes. And I'm not being coy. I'm just being realistic. Even that would cause enormous difficulties. I couldn't bring him back here—that would be taking too much advantage of Helen—and I couldn't spend my nights over at Robert's practice, where Ian lives.'

'That's true.' Sophie sighed. 'Perhaps you'd rather not be tied down here. You must put your personal life first. Don't risk your happiness for me. I'd hate to come between you and Ian.'

'I'm not going to let you down,' Joanna said firmly. 'Maybe Ian will find a solution. Meantime, nothing will happen. I'm not too keen on just having an affair and I know he isn't either. We'll probably do things the old-fashioned way.'

Sophie looked curious. 'Old-fashioned way—what do you mean?'

'Well—get engaged first, then get married. Not sleep together till then.'

Sophie raised her eyebrows sceptically. 'I can't see that happening.' Then she stopped. It was what she herself would choose to do, old-fashioned or not.

Joanna went on, 'Whatever happens, I'm going to stay with you and help to build up the practice till it's a going concern. Now let's talk about the party. How did you like Edward's nephew?'

'Not my cup of tea,' Sophie said briefly, and Joanna laughed.

'What is your cup of tea?' Without waiting for an answer, she added, 'Ian says——' then stopped as the telephone rang. 'Goodness! A call on Sunday. Things must be looking up.'

Sophie picked up the receiver, then her face froze. 'Yes,' she said curtly, 'we've got some, I think. I'll just have to make sure. Hold on, please.'

Putting the telephone down on the table, she turned to Joanna.

'It's Robert. He's run out of plaster and he's got an urgent call somewhere where he thinks he'll need it. We've got some, haven't we? That order that came in on Friday.'

'I'll go and see.' Joanna rushed off and Sophie stood looking down at the telephone. Her feelings were mixed. Much as she disliked having to talk to Robert, she knew she was bound to help. If she had been in a similar position she would also have called on the nearest colleague. Suddenly from the instrument she heard his voice. 'Hello—are you there?'

Reluctantly, she answered. 'Yes. Joanna has gone to the surgery to make sure.'

'Thank you.' There was a pause, then he spoke again, 'I'm going to ask another favour. This patient I have to see is a monkey with a suspected broken arm. I may need a bit of help. Ian is having the day off. He's fixed up to take someone out—Joanna, I think. So I'm wondering if you could possibly lend a hand.'

Sophie stifled a gasp. Of all the nerve! Well, this was obviously a job for Joanna, but. . . She frowned. Ian was taking her out. This was news. She hadn't mentioned it, but they had talked of other things.

She spoke into the receiver. 'I'm not sure. I rather think ——' She stopped as Joanna rushed into the room.

'OK,' she said breathlessly. 'We've got plenty.'

Putting her hand over the telephone, Sophie asked urgently, 'Are you going out with Ian today?'

'Oh, goodness! I forgot to tell you. We're meeting in an hour's time.' She looked anxious. 'If there's something special on, then of course I'll call it off.'

'Well, it's a monkey,' Sophie said. 'A suspected broken arm. Robert thinks he may need some help. He's asked me to go with him but if you'd rather. . .'

Joanna's face was a study. Torn in two by indecision, she reflected for a few moments, then said slowly, 'If it comes to choosing between Ian and a monkey, then Ian wins hands down. Do you mind?'

Turning back to the telephone, Sophie said coolly, 'All right. I'll come if it's really necessary.'

'Thank you. Bring the plaster and I'll be with you in about twenty minutes.'

'Just a moment. Give me the phone number so that Helen can pass on any message that might come in.'

She jotted it down, picked up the plaster from the surgery, then went to have a quick word with Helen. Suddenly she stopped dead. What was she doing? Going out with a man who, according to Dawn, was using her in order to achieve his own ends. Was he really in need of her help with this monkey? She drew a long breath. Well, she had been warned, so she would be on her guard.

Helen was surprised to hear about the case.

'There aren't any pet monkeys around here, I'm sure.' She pondered for a minute. 'I wonder if it's at the zoo over at Chesmore? I've only been there once — I took a friend with her small boy. Let me check the phone number.' Turning the pages of the telephone book, she soon found what she wanted. 'Yes, it's Chesmore Zoo. Well, well. Your Robert has got an important client there.'

'"My" Robert? He's not my Robert,' Sophie said indignantly.

'I'm sorry.' Helen looked confused. 'I shouldn't — well, it was at the party...' She stopped and bit her lip, then, seeing Sophie's colour rising, she added, 'Edward told me that he had seen you and Robert kissing out on the balcony.'

Sophie groaned inwardly. How could she explain this? She said quickly, 'Look, that's something I want to forget. I'll just say this. Robert Sheldrake is an unscrupulous man who will stop at nothing to get this practice. I've found it out now and I'm not going to let him get away with anything in future.'

'Yet you're going out with him now.' Helen frowned. 'I'm puzzled.'

'This is a professional thing. He needs help from another vet, and unfortunately I'm the only one available. The only link between us is a sick monkey.' Glancing at her watch, she said hurriedly, 'Look, I must fly. He'll be here in a minute. And, by the way, the reason I have to go is because Joanna is going out for the day with Ian Woodall.'

Helen stared. 'Curiouser and curiouser,' she said. 'What strange goings-on. I suppose you girls know what you're doing.'

Waiting in the surgery, Sophie was struck by a sudden thought. Why didn't Robert call on his veterinary nurse? Dawn was the obvious one to help him. She sighed with exasperation. This surely must be a trick, one to which she must find the answer before setting out with him. The sound of his car made her jump to her feet, and, picking up the plaster, she went out to meet him.

As Robert leaned over to open the passenger door, she handed him the plaster but made no attempt to get in. She said coldly, 'I've been thinking. You don't really need me. You have a veterinary nurse.'

He shook his head. 'Not today. Dawn has gone to visit her parents.'

'How unfortunate,' Sophie said sarcastically. 'Was she called away urgently?'

'I don't know why she went. She was entitled to a Sunday off duty.' Still holding the door open, he added impatiently, 'Well, are you coming? I'll have to anaesthetise this monkey if I have to set its arm, and I'm not sure of the capabilities of the Sunday staff.'

This seemed reasonable, so reluctantly Sophie got in his car and sat in silence as he drove out to the main road. At last he said, conversationally, 'We're going to Chesmore Zoo. They've asked me to do their veterinary work. The regular vet — a friend of mine — has gone to live in Australia and he recommended me to the zoo as his replacement. I've had experience of this kind of work. In my last job I used to look after the animals in a large zoo near the practice, where I was an assistant. It's interesting work and I learnt a lot.' He paused. 'That's the reason I decided to settle down here within easy reach of the zoo.'

That explained it, Sophie thought. His good luck was her bad luck. She said vehemently, 'I hate zoos. I think they should all be closed down.'

'They probably will be eventually. Meantime, someone has to look after the animals' health.' He paused. 'I don't like to see wild animals in captivity either.

Though, when you come to think of it, most of the animals in this country are in a kind of captivity. Cows, sheep, horses, pigs, dogs, cats, et cetera. They're mostly owned by us—some for companionship and others to be killed and eaten.'

Sophie shuddered. It was true, but hard to accept. They fell silent again, and, as they drove along, Sophie's thoughts grew more and more bewildered. Why was it that this man was such a pleasant and knowledgeable companion, and yet so hard and ruthless when it came to getting his own way? She sighed heavily, and then realised that her sigh was audible.

Robert said, 'I'm sorry if I've made you change any plans you had for today.'

'Well, actually I'm on duty. Joanna——' She stopped and he interrupted quickly.

'Ah, yes. This business with Ian. What are your thoughts on the subject?'

'Mixed.' Her answer was crisp, and she did not elaborate any further.

Undeterred, he went on, 'It complicates matters for both our practices. Do you think they are really seriously in love?'

She was startled by the direct question. Then, deciding to turn it to her own advantage, she said coldly, 'I don't know, but I think Joanna would be foolish to trust a man who is your friend.'

'That,' he said grimly, 'is quite uncalled-for. I suppose that's your way of punishing me for kissing you yesterday evening. I find it strange, because I was under the impression that. . .' He stopped and glanced across at her. 'What a lovely blush! Ah, well—I must have been mistaken. Perhaps if I try again I shall know for sure.'

She caught her breath. Then she said icily, 'I look upon that as a threat, not a promise.' She paused. 'And I don't like threats.'

Unexpectedly he sighed. Then he said quietly, 'In that case I must apologise.'

After a long silence, he pointed to a large house standing at the end of a long drive. 'Here we are,' he said. 'The zoo is at the back.'

A man came towards them as they pulled up, and Robert said, 'This is George—the head keeper. The manager lives in the house. He runs the business side and leaves the animals to George and the keepers who work with him.'

Introduced, Sophie listened with interest as George explained how the monkey had probably hurt his arm.

'It's the spot-nosed monkey. Nobody saw it happen, but I think most likely he was fighting and got caught up on something. He's sitting on his own now and whimpering. His arm is loose. I think you'll find it's broken.'

He led them towards what he called the monkey walk, where large cages of chattering inmates jumped about from branch to branch of trees and bushes in the enclosure. On one of them the poor little creature sat nursing his arm and looking very sorry for himself.

'He's an attractive little chap,' said the keeper. 'You can see why he has that odd name—that peculiar nose with its heart-shaped blob of white fur on the very end.'

Robert said, 'Well, let's see what we can do with that arm. Will you get him out, please? We must anaesthetise him.'

George nodded, picked up a net on a long pole, and went into the enclosure. To Sophie, the atmosphere of the zoo was absorbing, but what pleased her most was the way in which Robert was including her in what he had to do. When the keeper had captured the monkey in the net he led the way to a small building which he informed them was the annexe to the quarantine block. Then, as he placed the net on the table, the wildly chattering monkey grew quiet. As Robert prepared a syringe he said, 'I'm going to put the injection in through the net.' He indicated the monkey's thigh. He turned to the keeper. 'Try and keep him still, will you?'

Expertly held, the monkey began whimpering again, his sad eyes looking at them imploringly, and Sophie's heart was wrung with pity. Quickly Robert inserted the needle into the thigh muscle, and in about a minute, the small body went limp. Taking off the net, Robert felt the reflexes then examined the arm and drew Sophie to inspect the damage.

'It's broken all right,' he said. 'Here, on the lower end of the humerus, just above the elbow. No need for an X-ray. We'll put it in plaster.'

'I thought you might,' said the keeper. 'There's a bowl of water here for you.'

Taking the roll of plaster from Sophie, Robert placed it in the water, then, pulling the broken limb out straight, he lined up the bones and set the arm.

'Now——' he turned to Sophie '—will you hold it, please, and keep up the tension while I put on the plaster? As you know, I must be quick or it will go hard.'

She watched, as, starting at the shoulder, he wound it right down the arm and the hand, covering the fingers, then wound it back up to the shoulder again. While he was doing a little more manipulation of the bones before the plaster set, she got ready an injection of antibiotic and he took it from her with a nod of approval. At last he stood back satisfied, and the keeper asked, 'How long will he have to keep it on?'

'Three weeks at least, and he must stay here for that time. When I take the plaster off, that's when your problems will begin.'

'Why's that?' Sophie looked perplexed, but the keeper nodded ruefully.

'We shall then have to find somewhere else for him to live. Probably with a different species. After he's been kept on his own, the troop won't accept him back.'

Sophie frowned. 'Why do monkeys fight so much?'

George was evidently used to this question and he said patiently, 'In the natural state, they live in colonies with separate family groups and, like all families, they fall out with each other from time to time. If one attacks another, the weaker one runs away and comes back when the trouble is over. But in captivity there's nowhere for them to run, so it's up to us to see they don't hurt each other badly.'

Sophie nodded, keeping to herself the thought that George was expounding a powerful argument against the keeping of animals in zoos.

She watched as Robert tested the plaster.

'It's hard now,' he said, 'so you can put him in a cage. Tomorrow I'll come and have another look at him.' As they walked back to the car, Sophie asked, 'Do you pay a regular visit here or do you wait until they call you?'

'I do a weekly round of all the inmates. I like to study them — very often I can see something the keepers wouldn't necessarily notice. There's nearly always some problem or other. It's very interesting work, although quite a lot of it is elementary. For instance, you could have treated that monkey yourself if it had been brought into your surgery. But the novelty of zoo work lies in the variety of patients. Different species, different anatomies. Anything from tigers to tortoises.'

Sophie laughed. Then, impulsively, forgetting the differences that divided them, she said, 'I'm glad I came with you. It was very instructive.'

He glanced at her quickly as he opened his car door.

'Well, how about sometimes coming with me when I do my inspection?'

She hesitated as caution returned. The invitation was enticing. The prospect of enlarging her experience was strong. But was it worth the risk of sharing work with the rival practice? She pondered for a minute. Why not? She could always stop going when she wanted. She began to speak, but he said, with a shrug, 'I can see you don't want to get too involved, so perhaps we'd better forget it.'

'Oh, no!' She was dismayed. 'I'd like to take up your offer. I can arrange my work accordingly.'

He looked pleased, took a quick glance at his watch, and said, 'Let's drink to that. There's a nice little pub on the way back.'

She shook her head. This was going too far. 'Sorry. I must get back. I'm on duty. Joanna——'

'Yes, of course. The two love-birds. Problems ahead.'

She stiffened. 'They'll come to some arrangement. Joanna won't let me down.'

He shrugged disbelievingly. 'I don't see how she can avoid it. Ian is determined not to let her go, and even if they don't get married they'll almost certainly become lovers, which will make things extremely awkward.'

Sophie said coolly. 'It's nothing to do with us how they conduct their affairs.'

'You don't think so?' His tone was sceptical. 'You can't know much about the ups and downs of love and passion if you think that.'

With her eyes fixed on the road ahead, she frowned. This conversation was getting too intimate — the very thing she wanted to avoid. She said, 'I'm sure they'll sort things out, in spite of your hints of trouble ahead.'

'I'm not hinting at anything. I'm speaking from experience. A relationship without a foundation of marriage is always unstable. I may be old-fashioned, but I'd rather see them married than indulging in a sordid little affair.'

'There's nothing sordid about it.' Sophie's voice trembled. 'If they think it's OK to become lovers, then it will be OK. It depends on their characters and their beliefs.'

He was silent for a minute, and she began to hope he had lost interest in the subject. Then he asked suddenly, 'Do you also speak from experience?'

She drew a quick breath. 'That's nothing to do with you, and it's an impertinent question.'

'Well, that's no answer.' He paused. 'Or perhaps it is.'

She said nothing, but her colour rose. Determined to change the conversation, she opened her mouth to make a remark about the surrounding countryside, but he said suddenly, 'It's too much to hope that a beautiful girl like you has had no experience. I assume——'

'You've no right to assume anything about me,' she

snapped, then added recklessly, 'Just because some girls sleep around, it doesn't mean to say we all do.'

'You mean to say. . .' He half turned to look at her, then, as he saw her heightened colour, he said quietly, 'I'm sorry. I didn't mean to pry.'

She blinked hard. She felt ridiculed, despised for her lack of worldliness. But what right had he to probe into her personal life? With growing anger, she decided to retaliate. She said, 'You obviously think of yourself as one of the world's great lovers. Is Dawn one of your many conquests? She implied that she had a right to you last night.'

As soon as the words were out, she could have bitten her tongue, but it was too late. He said slowly, 'I'm glad you haven't forgotten last night. I haven't either. As for Dawn — well, that has nothing to do with you.'

'She seemed to think otherwise. She said you were using me just as she had been used. Anything to get my practice, in fact.'

'She has not been used,' he said raspingly. 'She expected more than I was prepared to give. As for doing anything to get your practice — good God! What do you think I am?' He swerved violently and, as she gasped, he said, 'Stop needling me. Do you want to have an accident?'

She said no more and as soon as they arrived at Broom House she said, 'No need to take me right up to the house — I can walk up the drive.'

He took no notice, but turned in and drew up in the courtyard. Then, as Sophie prepared to get out, she saw an empty car — a blue Porsche — standing outside the surgery door. Wondering who the wealthy client was, she began to hurry, but Robert's voice stopped her.

'That's Giles Brandon's car,' he said. 'No doubt you'll find his company more pleasant than mine. I suppose you knew he'd be here and that's why you wanted me to drop you off?'

Glimpsed through the window, she could see Helen and Giles standing by the surgery table, and the worried expression on Helen's face told its own tale. She turned to Robert. 'It's obviously an emergency case. I must see to it. Thank you for the zoo visit.'

As she hastened towards the surgery she suddenly realised that Robert was behind her. Catching her up, he said, 'You may want help. Joanna's not here, Helen is no veterinary nurse, and Giles will be useless.'

Her first impulse was to make him turn back, then common sense prevailed. It depended on the case, of course, and she hoped fervently that it would be something she could manage on her own. But perhaps. . . She opened the surgery door and Helen greeted her with a great sigh of relief. Pointing to the miniature poodle on the table, she said, 'This is Edward's housekeeper's dog—well, bitch. She's in a bad way trying to have her pups. She must have been straining all day. Mrs Baxter says she was so busy with the cleaning-up after the party that she didn't pay much attention, thought everything would progress naturally. Then a short time ago she came to Edward in a great state.' She paused for breath and Giles took up the tale.

'She thinks Yvette may be dying. My uncle told me to bring her to you and we've been here about twenty minutes.' He looked at Sophie reproachfully, 'No one on duty, so I rang the other practice. . .' He frowned at Robert, 'No one there either. I thought vets were supposed to be on twenty-four-hour call.'

He was right, of course, as Sophie acknowledged ruefully to herself but Robert said stiffly, 'When you rang my surgery, the answering-machine gave the zoo number. Why didn't you ring there?'

Giles shrugged. 'No point. You were obviously busy there.' He turned to Sophie. 'What I can't understand is that Helen told me the same thing. You were also at the zoo, she said.' He added meaningly, with a sideways glance at Robert, 'With him.'

Robert's eyes glinted angrily, but he ignored Giles and, joining Sophie at the table, he said, 'You'll need help. It will have to be a Caesarean.'

She nodded, as she looked down at the tiny poodle. Eyes half-closed, swollen body limp and almost lifeless, the poodle certainly seemed near to death.

'I'll just feel the cervix,' she said, and as Yvette became aware of the gentle examination, she opened her eyes and gave a doleful little whimper.

'All her straining has been useless,' Sophie said. 'There's nothing in the passage, so that means a dead puppy, I'm afraid. Risky to do a Caesarean in her state of exhaustion, but there's no option now.' She paused. 'What on earth possessed Mrs Baxter to let such a tiny bitch be mated?'

'Oh, that.' Giles shrugged indifferently. 'She must have got out when she was in season.'

Sophie frowned. 'Well, leave her to me. I'll do my best.'

Giles looked rather shamefaced. 'I'd like to offer to help, but I'm afraid I'm one of those people who faint at the sight of blood.'

Sophie smiled. 'Certainly no use to me. In any case, I can manage.'

'With a little help from a friend,' Robert murmured,

and Sophie turned. About to refuse any assistance, she forced back her pride and nodded in reluctant acceptance.

'I'll go and report to Mrs Baxter,' said Giles, and Helen sighed with relief.

'Well, thank goodness for that. I'll go back and finish cooking lunch.'

It didn't take much anaesthetic to render the exhausted patient unconscious, and, as Sophie made the first incision, she put aside her dislike of being critically watched by her professional rival and concentrated on her life-saving task. The first puppy was lifted out dead, and as she handed it over Robert said, 'What a size. No wonder she couldn't pass it.'

Sophie said quickly. 'There's one more—I think it's still got a spark of life.'

Half an hour later, the puppy saved, Yvette was still unconscious and Sophie studied her breathing anxiously.

'I gave her a very light anaesthetic—there should be some response from her reflexes by now.' She paused. 'I'll stay here and watch her. Thank you for your help, but I mustn't keep you any longer.'

Robert shook his head. 'I'm too interested to go. Have you got the heart stimulant?'

'Over there.' She pointed to the drug shelf and he took the bottle out, filled a syringe, and handed it to her. Then, as soon as the injection was in, he said, 'How about a cup of something—coffee or tea? It's quite a long time since breakfast.'

It seemed a good idea, but Sophie hesitated. Just so long as the two of them were involved professionally, she was at ease with him, but once that link was severed, she could only feel antagonism towards him.

Dawn's words re-echoed in her mind, in spite of the fact that Robert had derided them so vehemently, and she felt that she must always be on her guard. But already she had been to the zoo with him and accepted an invitation for future visits. Into the bargain he had taken part in her own work in her practice while Joanna was involved with his assistant. The situation was becoming dangerous. She shook her head, 'No. I don't want anything to drink. Why don't you go back to your surgery? You heard what Giles said about vets being available all day and night.'

'Giles is an idiot,' he said angrily. 'He could have contacted me if he had tried.' He paused. 'I expect he's just jealous of the fact that we were out together.'

'Jealous?' Sophie stopped in the act of tidying up the table. 'What on earth makes you say that?'

He smiled cynically. 'Don't pretend not to understand. He's a man and I'm a man, and you are a distractingly beautiful girl. It's a classic situation.'

'Don't be stupid!' Tense with anger at first, she suddenly burst into scornful laughter. 'Well, yes, perhaps it is a classic situation. One of you tries to lure me with promises of future riches and the other is only interested in what I possess — namely a practice that is a thorn in his flesh. Well, I'm not fooled that easily. I can see right through you both.'

Her mocking laughter stopped suddenly as she saw his face go deathly white. Without another word, he turned and went out of the room. A moment later she heard his car turning in the courtyard, then the sound faded as he drove away.

CHAPTER SIX

ALONE in the surgery Sophie continued her watch over her patient until at last the signs of recovery appeared. She waited until she was completely satisfied, then she relaxed and her thoughts returned to Robert. Maybe she had been too outspoken, but she had only stated the truth. Obviously he hadn't liked it, because it showed that she understood his motives only too well. Nevertheless the memory of his stricken face was somehow disturbing and made her feel guilty—a strange and unpleasant sensation that she tried to banish by taking a final look at her patient. Satisfied, she picked up the telephone and rang through to Edward's house, hoping the housekeeper would answer. Rather to her disappointment, Giles replied, and when she gave him the news about Yvette she added cautiously, 'Mind you, she still has a little way to go yet, but I think she'll be OK.'

'What a clever girl you are. Will you let me take you out to dinner tomorrow in gratitude for what you've done?'

'I don't know why you should feel gratitude,' Sophie said coolly. 'Yvette doesn't belong to you.'

'Ah, but think of the weeping and wailing my uncle and I would have had to endure if you hadn't used your skill to save the wretched poodle. Now Mrs Baxter will be her old self again and life will continue smoothly.'

Sophie laughed. 'A typical man's point of view.'

'Oh, Sophie, don't be so unkind.' His voice was pleasantly cajoling. 'Take pity on a lonely bachelor. I'd love to take you out. I know of a very nice hotel in Seabourne where we can enjoy a fabulous meal and afterwards take a romantic stroll by the sea in the moonlight.'

She said lightly, 'The meal sounds tempting, but I'm not so sure about the moonlight stroll.'

'Sophie — is there no romance in your scientific soul?'

She paused before replying. This light-hearted banter was amusing, but she mustn't let it get out of hand. Giles, in spite of his charm, was not the type of man she admired, still less the type with whom she could fall in love. Somewhere at the back of her mind, she knew there was an image of someone, but she dare not look too closely. Better to distract herself with Giles. Besides, his invitation sounded attractive.

'Sophie — are you still there? Will you come or not?'

'Yes,' she said recklessly. 'I'll come. I could manage tomorrow after surgery. Say about seven-thirty.' She paused. 'That's if nothing happens to make me cry off.'

'What an elusive girl you are. Still I suppose I have to take second place to your work.'

'Definitely.' She felt light-headed and wondered why. Was it because of what Robert had said about Giles being jealous? Putting down the telephone, she tried to sort out her motive for promising to go out with Giles. Was she now trying to make Robert jealous in his turn? If so, why? Suddenly her heart jerked as the answer came like a flash of lightning. For one startled moment she felt the shock, then resolutely she shook it off. It couldn't be true. It was just a dangerous fantasy.

Keeping a tight hold on herself, she went in search

of Helen and accepted with gratitude her invitation to lunch.

It was not until they were drinking coffee that Helen said, 'Well, now that you've told me all about your visit to the zoo, tell me what you think about Joanna and Ian Woodall.'

'Well, this is the situation. . .' Sophie began, and when she had finished Helen sat in silence for a few minutes. At last she said,

'One can only be glad for their sakes. I don't know Ian, but I do know Joanna, and you couldn't have a more loyal friend. So I see no need to worry. Whichever they choose, we must accept it.' She paused. 'Of course, it will change things a bit. You know, I can't help thinking that one day your practice and that of Robert Sheldrake's will have to merge.'

Sophie sat up, looking appalled. 'How can you say such a thing? I'd rather pack up here altogether and take a job as an assistant again. Mind you, things would have to be very bad indeed before I'd do that.' Then, seeing her godmother's sceptical smile, she deliberately changed the subject and spoke of the poodle. She added, 'It was Edward who told Giles to bring Yvette to me. I appreciate that.'

Helen nodded. 'Yes, it gives an undoubted boost to your practice. Mrs Baxter will spread the glad news. By the way, how do you like Giles?'

Sophie lifted her shoulders. 'He's all right. As a matter of fact, he's taking me out to dinner tomorrow.'

'Well, that's good news. Edward will be pleased.'

Sophie looked puzzled. 'Why? What's it got to do with him?'

Helen laughed. 'He'd like Giles to get married and thinks you'd be just the right girl for him.'

'You're joking! The old matchmaker!'

'Not so much of the "old",' Helen said reprovingly. 'He's only fifty-seven — two years my senior. Naturally he'd like Giles to get married and produce an heir for his estate.'

'Well, he's only got to do what a lot of older men do — marry a young girl and produce an heir himself.'

'Oh, yes. He could do that, but. . .' Helen paused and her mouth flickered into a smile. 'I rather think he wants me to marry him, and I'm too old to have the necessary child.'

'Goodness!' Sophie gazed at her godmother, saw the pretty flush on her cheeks, and said cautiously, 'I never thought you'd marry again. Not after. . .' She left the phrase unfinished and Helen nodded calmly.

'You're quite right. I said once was enough, didn't I? Well, I shall need a lot of persuasion to change my mind, but I've known Edward for a very long time and we're good friends. Sometimes friendship is a sound basis for a good marriage.'

Sophie mused aloud, 'Very practical. Not at all romantic.'

'I'm past the age for romance.' Helen smiled, but her colour belied the words. Deftly turning the conversation, she said, 'Betty tells me the village people are very intrigued by the two veterinary practices here, and Joanna wouldn't be too pleased if she knew that they are firmly under the impression that you only do small animals and Robert and Ian are large-animal vets.' She paused. 'No need to frown, Sophie. I think it's a good thing. It may not be exactly what you planned, but sometimes one must compromise. It's logical that two male vets should get most of the farm work.'

Sophie nodded reluctantly. Then, brightening up,

she said, 'One good thing—I've got the pet shop. I'm going there tomorrow after surgery. I'm looking foward to it.'

'That's very useful. Now I've remembered something else, also from Betty. She knows the woman who cleans for the Sheldrake practice, and the other day, while waiting in the bus shelter, they got talking about Dawn and Robert. Apparently the cleaner overheard them having a tremendous row. Dawn accused him——'

'I don't want to know,' Sophie interrupted sharply, then, seeing that Helen looked rather ruffled, she added in a more conciliatory tone, 'It's just that, although I'm very interested in what goes on in that practice on the veterinary side, I don't really think we ought to interest ourselves in the personal ups and downs of the people working there.' She flushed as she met the quizzical expression in Helen's eyes. 'That sounds very smug, doesn't it? The thing is that I want to keep the distance between us as far apart as possible. You do understand, don't you?'

Helen nodded slowly, her eyes fixed searchingly on Sophie's troubled face. 'Oh, yes,' she said meaningly. 'I understand, I understand very well.'

Next morning Sophie and Joanna had a busy surgery. Several patients were rather recalcitrant, but Helen seemed able to control them when a little assistance became necessary. At one point, however, her usual calm manner deserted her. A tame rabbit was brought in with a large abscess about the size of an egg on its cheek. It tried to jump off the table and had to be held firmly so that Sophie could freeze the surrounding area before lancing it. Then, as the revolting mess began to ooze out, Helen drew back and shut her eyes. For a moment she looked quite faint, but with a great effort she stood her ground. Sophie said sympathetically, 'I know it's horrible, but it must be done.'

'Of course it must.' Helen was apologetic. 'Don't mind me. I'll get used to these things in time.'

Sophie finished draining the abscess and injected a liquid antibiotic into the cavity, then she handed the rabbit over to Helen, who took it out to the small boy in the waiting-room. Coming back, she said, 'Seeing that child's face was a revelation. Your work is so rewarding, even though it's unpleasant at times. I'm glad to be able to help, even in a small way.'

When the next case came in, Helen proved her worth. A large Boxer dog resisted wildly being put on the table in order to have his nails trimmed. He made such noisy protestations that his nervous owner fled back into the waiting-room. At last, yielding to Helen's firm manner, he gradually calmed down. Even then the task was difficult, and Sophie breathed a sigh of relief when it was done.

'The simplest things are sometimes the most difficult to treat,' she remarked. 'That took much longer than I would have believed.' She glanced at her watch. 'I must get moving soon. I told Mr Miller at the pet shop I'd be there soon after surgery.'

'I can carry on here with Helen's assistance — that is, if I'm not called away,' Joanna said, but she had no sooner spoken than the telephone rang. They waited as she answered it, then, after a few words, she put the instrument back and grinned triumphantly.

'A horse with colic. Another new client. It's only just up the road, so I'll probably be back soon.'

Sophie looked doubtful. 'Colic cases are uncertain.

You could be ages. Let's see who's left in the waiting-room.'

A woman was sitting there, but with no pet beside her. At the sound of Sophie's entry, she turned quickly and stood facing her.

'Dawn!' Sophie exclaimed. 'What on earth. . .?'

The veterinary nurse stared back at her and gave a short laugh. 'Surprise, surprise,' she said mockingly, then her voice changed. 'I've come to talk to you. It's important. I want to clear things up.'

Sophie was nonplussed. This looked like being a dramatic confrontation as, judging from the strained expression on Dawn's face, she was very much on edge.

'Well, I can't talk now. I have an urgent appointment in Seabourne. It will have to wait. This afternoon, perhaps? Things will be quieter then.'

Dawn frowned. 'Surely you can spare me ten minutes — say a quarter of an hour?'

'I'm afraid not — I really must go. It's urgent.'

'A client in Seabourne. You must be doing quite well. You've been busy doing this surgery, too.'

Sophie moved towards the door and Dawn shrugged. 'All right. I'll come over after lunch. About two o'clock. I shouldn't really be here now, but we had a very quiet surgery. No one there, in fact. We don't have an afternoon surgery, so I'll have more time to talk.'

As she went away, Sophie rushed back to the others, picked up her case, and said quickly, 'That was Dawn. Can't think what she wants. She's coming back this afternoon.'

She left Helen and Joanna staring open-mouthed, and as she got into her car she was as puzzled as they were. She pondered for a while, then, as the traffic towards Seabourne became heavier, she abandoned the subject and concentrated on her driving.

Mr Miller greeted her cheerfully.

'Fifteen puppies to be done with the first injection. They're all under twelve weeks old, so they will only be able to have the measles and Parvo injection. Did you bring the vaccination cards?'

'Oh! My goodness!' Sophie put her hand to her head. 'I came away in such a hurry—I've forgotten.' She stopped as she saw the look of annoyance on his face. 'I'm terribly sorry—I'll go back and get them.'

'No, don't do that. I've got a customer coming in who wants to choose a puppy, and it must be vaccinated before it leaves here. I'll have to tell him that I'll post the card on to him. You can bring them in this afternoon and fill them in here. Now, come and see them.'

As she followed him to the back of the shop, Sophie remembered with sharp dismay the appointment she had made with Dawn. Somehow or other, she must get the cards to Mr Miller and be back to the surgery by two o'clock. Just so long as no emergency came up. . . She certainly didn't want to cut short this visit to the pet shop, where Mr Miller had promised to tell her more about his stock of animals.

The puppies were entrancing—English springer spaniels with silky coats, long, soft ears and beautiful, intelligent eyes, three German shepherds showing promise of becoming magnificent animals, Yorkshire terriers, timid and appealing, with their sharp little eyes gazing out from under their long hair, and two Jack Russell terriers, already boisterous and full of life. Mr Miller said, 'You can see that they are all good specimens. As I told you, they're from the best breeders — those whose kennels have passed inspection.'

Sophie nodded as she finished examining the last one. Then, as she began to prepare the injections, Mr Miller added, 'I'll make a list for my records, along with dates, but I shan't be able to sell any until I have the vaccination cards. Don't forget to stamp them with your address.'

She could see that he was still slightly irritated by her forgetfulness. It was to be expected, and she knew she must show herself to be more efficient in future. Making a mental note not to let outside interests interfere with her work, she began to inject the puppies. Mr Miller held each one up in turn, and as she slipped in the needle skilfully they scarcely noticed the momentary discomfort.

Mr Miller finished writing down the details and said ruefully, 'I was going to give you coffee and then a tour round the rest of my animals, but there's no time left.'

Sophie looked thoughtful. 'If I may use your telephone, then I'll ring my surgery and get someone to bring the vaccination cards in right now.'

He nodded and she tapped out the number. Helen answered and sounded so anxious that Sophie grew apprehensive.

'No, I can't come. Joanna is still out and I've got a client here with a cat. A possible broken leg. I can't send her away — she's come in from Chesmore.'

Sophie relayed the information to Mr Miller, who shrugged irritably and told her to be as quick as possible, but the traffic was heavy as she drove out of the town and all the time she was praying that the cat's leg would not be really broken. Perhaps Joanna would be back and able to deal with it. At last she reached

Broom House and rushed into the surgery, where Helen greeted her with evident relief.

'Mrs Benson has been here waiting very patiently,' she said, and, after apologising to her client, Sophie set to work.

She examined the cat slowly and carefully, not allowing herself to be distracted by the thought of Mr Miller waiting irritably for the vaccination cards or her future appointment with Dawn. The patient immediately under her care must have priority, and as always she was able to give full attention to her diagnosis. At last she looked up and smiled at the cat's owner.

'No bones broken, I can assure you. It's badly bruised — it may have been knocked by a car. Whatever the cause, there's no need for you to worry. This is what I'll do — an injection to take away the pain and reduce the bruising and a few tablets for you to give today and tomorrow. It should be OK by then.'

It was quite a problem to cut short her client's long-winded story of the cat's movements during the last twenty-four hours, but at last the door closed and Sophie turned to Helen.

'I hope I wasn't too curt with her, but I've got to get back to Seabourne with the vaccination cards. I'm angry with myself for forgetting them.'

'It wasn't surprising in view of the unexpected visitor you had just before you left.'

Sophie looked up from counting out the vaccination cards.

'I've had to put her off till two o'clock. Unfortunately Mr Miller wants to show me round his shop, and that will take some time. I only hope I can make it.' She looked around. 'Where's the rubber stamp with our name and address on it?'

A hurried search revealed its whereabouts, then at last Sophie was ready to leave.

Driving once more as fast as she dared, she soon reached the pet shop and saw that Mr Miller was occupied with a customer. He gave her a quick nod of approval and she went down to the end of the shop and began filling in the certificates, taking her information from the records Mr Miller had already made. As she stamped the last one she glanced at her watch. Then, getting up, she went to the telephone and signalled to Mr Miller for permission to use it. He nodded and she tapped out the Sheldrake practice number. To her dismay, Robert himself answered, but, ignoring this stroke of bad luck, she asked calmly if she could speak to Dawn.

'I'm afraid she's out at the moment,' he said. 'That's Sophie speaking, isn't it? I'd know your voice anywhere. Can I take a message?'

'No — well, yes. Would you mind telling her that I'm in Seabourne and I think I'm going to be late for our appointment at two o'clock? Three o'clock would be better.'

'Appointment with Dawn? What's going on?'

Annoyed with his curiosity, she said sharply, 'Nothing is "going on", as you put it. Dawn has asked to have a talk with me. I don't know any more than that.'

'Well, well. I'll pass the message on. I can't help wondering, though. . .' He gave a short laugh just as she rang off.

'Well, now. . .' Mr Miller stood behind her. 'A quick cup of coffee, then I'll show you round.'

He seemed to have recovered his good humour. He asked her how things were going in her practice and fixed up a regular day for her to do vaccinations and inspect the other species. She said laughingly, 'It's rather like a mini zoo, isn't it? I went round Chesmore Zoo the other day and found it fascinating.'

He was interested. 'I suppose you went round as a visitor—they'd have their own vet, naturally.'

Suddenly Sophie found she was in deep water. She had no wish to praise up Robert's practice, but, having already told Mr Miller so much of her ambitions and the problems she faced, it would be foolish to appear evasive. She said at last, 'You may think it strange, but I went round with Mr Sheldrake. He's been appointed the zoo vet.'

'You went round with him—your rival? Yes, that is a bit odd.' He paused, then came out with the inevitable suggestion that she found so irritating. 'Why don't your two practices join up? Amalgamate instead of fighting each other. Looking at it from a businessman's point of view, it's the obvious thing to do. Look at me—I have a thriving shop in Westmead and now I've opened up here in Seabourne. Anyone who tried to set up in between us would find it hard going. And, of course, you and Mr Sheldrake are so close to each other that it's ridiculous to be in opposition. I'm surprised that the idea hasn't occurred to either of you.'

'It's occurred to him,' she said bitterly. 'He'd very much like to take over, but it's the last thing I want.'

'I said amalgamate—not take over. However——' he grinned at the expression on her face '—I'd better not say any more. But mark my words—it'll happen one day.' He paused again and eyed her keenly. 'Of course, if you resist long enough you may be able to lay down all sorts of conditions to which, if he's so keen, he'll have to agree. That's probably the best way.'

Inwardly Sophie was furious, but she merely shrugged, finished her coffee and waited until he got up. Leading her to the front of the shop, he said, 'This is very small fry compared with Chesmore Zoo, but it covers most of all the species that we are allowed to sell. Apart from dogs and cats, we have hamsters, guinea pigs, rabbits, budgies, canaries, cockatoos, Amazon parrots, macaws, African cockatiels, finches and parakeets—I'm sure you know how to treat them. Then there are chinchillas and ferrets, which no doubt you often inject against TB and distemper, and over there we've rats, mice, gerbils and chipmunks.' He stopped beside a glass cage and, involuntarily, Sophie drew back. He laughed. 'Spiders—tarantulas. Yes, you look surprised, but lots of people keep them as. . . well——' he shrugged 'hardly as pets, but probably because they like to have something different.' Turning, he grinned at the apprehension she could hardly hide. 'Don't worry. You won't be called upon to give them injections.' He moved on. 'Now, snakes. As you know, they sometimes get mouth rot and occasionally they get mites under their scales, rather like dogs and cats get fleas. An insecticide soon deals with all that. By the way, I don't keep any poisonous snakes. Now here are the lizards—great favourites with small boys— and here are terrapins, as you can see, they're water creatures. No tortoises of course. There is now a ban on importing them.' He paused. 'Tropical fish—I expect you know how to deal with them. Well, what do you think?' He looked at her questioningly. 'Will you be able to cope?'

Sophie drew a long breath, 'You have a great variety,

but my veterinary training covers most of all these species. It's mainly a question of studying their lifestyle, common sense, and, of course, antibiotics.' She paused, then added thoughtfully, 'What we should do without antibiotics I can't imagine. The number of lives saved since their discovery is almost incredible.'

Thinking it over as she drove back, Sophie was conscious of mixed feelings. She was no longer anxious about her ability to cope with the inmates of the pet shop, but she still disliked the sight of birds and some of the more sensitive animals being kept in captivity.

And what would be the fate of these creatures once they were sold to well-meaning but probably ignorant people? That, she knew full well, she could do nothing about, although she disapproved of the whole set-up. Her only duty was, as Robert had said about the zoo, to look after their health and welfare.

Pulling up outside her surgery, she looked at her watch. Only one-thirty. She needn't have changed Dawn's appointment after all. Still, it would give her time to discuss the subject over a sandwich with Joanna.

'I can't imagine what she wants,' Joanna said, 'unless, having quarelled with Robert, she's going to ask you for a job.'

They were both laughing when Helen walked in and demanded to be enlightened. Then she said thoughtfully, 'I wonder if she's going to warn you off Robert. Don't look so incredulous, Sophie. It must have occurred to you that Dawn is probably very jealous — in particular of the fact that he took you with him to the zoo.'

Not willing to admit that she had had the same idea, Sophie said cautiously, 'Dawn wasn't available to help him with the monkey. It was purely a professional emergency.'

'Could he really not have managed without you?'

Sophie shrugged. 'Probably. But he didn't know whether the Sunday staff would be up to it.'

Helen looked mildly sceptical. 'Well, you'll soon find out, but to my mind Dawn has grounds for jealousy. Do let me know how you get on with her. I'm all agog.'

When she had gone, Joanna said, 'I'm inclined to think Helen is right. Would you like me to be within reach in case Dawn turns nasty?'

'Don't be absurd.' Sophie burst out laughing, then proceeded to describe her visit to the pet shop. Joanna was pleased to hear about it, then she said,

'We're doing better and better, aren't we? I've just got two more clients. First of all, the owners of the horse with colic—I was lucky there. It recovered quickly after I gave it an injection. Then Mr Jarvis had a friend with him when I went out to deal with piglets who were scouring, and this man owns a smallholding near by. A few pigs, a couple of horses, half a dozen bullocks—you know the kind of set-up. He watched me deal with the piglets and said he would call me when he needed a vet.' She stopped and went to look out of the window. 'Here comes Dawn, walking up the drive—I'd better disappear.' She grinned. 'If she attacks you, just scream. I'll be on the alert.'

Sophie found it hard to suppress a smile as she greeted her visitor, but there was no smile on Dawn's face. Ushering her into the office, Sophie offered coffee, but a shake of the head was Dawn's only response. As soon as she was seated, she said in a voice that was hard and tense, 'You must know why I've come.'

'No, I simply haven't a clue,' Sophie said calmly. 'You made it sound important, and I've been racking my brains ever since.'

'Don't give me that,' Dawn said derisively. 'It's no use playing the innocent with me. I know you're after Robert, but, although you may think you'll succeed, I'm here to warn you.'

Sophie stared, speechless for a moment, then she said coldly, 'Very kind of you, but it's quite unnecessary. In the first place, I'm not, as you put it so vividly, "after" Robert. In the second, I can't imagine what you have to warn me about.'

'I'm warning you not to fall into his trap. I told you on Saturday evening that he's using you, just as he's used me.'

A sudden chill swept over Sophie, but she said evenly, 'I don't know what he's done to you. That's not my affair. As for me, I'm not easily fooled by anyone, least of all by Robert Sheldrake. If that's all you've come to say——' She stood up and went to open the door, but stopped when Dawn burst out,

'I'll tell you what he's done to me. He brought me down here to work for him under false pretences. We were on the verge of an affair, but the moment he met you everything came to a dead stop. And, knowing him so well, I could see his little game. He covets your practice, and in order to get it he'll play the same trick on you that he played on me.'

Sophie pulled the door open. 'I don't want to hear any more. You're obviously imagining a situation that doesn't exist.'

Dawn got up slowly. Pale and calmer now, she looked at Sophie searchingly. 'Well, on your own head be it. I've done my best. Of course, if you tell him what

I've said he'll deny it, but I assure you he only wants one thing and that's your practice.'

Sophie shut the door behind her and found herself trembling. Sinking into a chair, she stared ahead unseeingly. Gradually she began to analyse her emotions and found, to her surprise, that uppermost in her mind was a feeling of pity for Dawn. A broken relationship was always sad, but the idea that she, Sophie, was responsible was absurd. At last, pulling herself together, she went to give Joanna and Helen a watered-down version of the scene that had just taken place — watered-down because, for some subconscious reason, she felt that Dawn's story was not quite believable. Robert Sheldrake's character could surely not be as black as Dawn had painted.

CHAPTER SEVEN

WHEN Sophie woke on Tuesday morning she remembered with something of a shock that she had promised to go out to dinner with Giles. Joanna greeted the news with surprise.

'I thought you weren't too keen on him.'

'Well, it will make a break.' Sophie shrugged indifferently. 'He's promised me a fabulous dinner, to say nothing of what he calls 'a romantic stroll by the sea in the moonlight.' She laughed at the expression on Joanna's face, then gave a little frown. 'Actually I rather wish I hadn't agreed. I think I'm going to be bored. A little of Giles goes a long way. Still, I can't get out of it now.'

Joanna grinned mischievously, 'Oh, yes, you could. One of the advantages of being a vet is that we can get out of almost anything by pleading an emergency. But you're too scrupulous for that, aren't you?'

Sophie laughed. 'Poor old Giles. I can't play that sort of trick on him—besides, I'd only have to agree to another date.' She looked at the clock. 'Nearly surgery time. Let's hope it'll be a busy one.'

The waiting-room was moderately full and there were several clients who had come in from neighbouring villages. Joanna gave a thumbs-up sign when the last one left.

'Like Topsy, the practice just grows and grows,' she said. 'I've got to go out and you've got two cats to spay.' She turned as Helen came into the room. 'Here's your veterinary nurse — you won't need my help.'

Helen laughed. 'I don't think I'm worthy of that title, but I am getting used to seeing unpleasant sights. Really, I'm surprised that there is so little blood with these operations.'

'Well, clamps on the arteries stop that,' Sophie said, and Joanna added reminiscently,

'I remember on one occasion, soon after I began operating, cutting into an artery by mistake, and a great spurt of blood like a fountain came up into my face. It was terrifying to a novice, but quite easy to deal with. Ian was telling me ——' She stopped abruptly and her colour rose. 'I'm sorry. I ought not to talk about him to you. I don't suppose you're overjoyed that I've got a friend in the rival camp.'

'Don't be silly — I thought we had settled all that.' Sophie paused, then asked hesitantly, 'How are things going with you and Ian?'

Joanna spoke softly, with one eye on Helen, who had gone to sterilise the instruments. 'It's all marvellous. The only problem is that Ian wants to get married and I don't.'

'Why not? Surely if you love each other ——'

'You know why not. I told you I'd put things off until this practice is going strong. Even then. . .' She paused and looked down at her coffee, twisting the mug round and round. 'Well — I don't like to think about it. Ian says we both ought to leave and either take up work as a married couple in another practice with a view of eventual partnership or set up on our own somewhere, a good long way from here, of course. But I won't leave you in the lurch even if that time comes. I would always stay until you had found someone to replace me.'

Sophie nodded slowly, then Helen came up to the table.

'I couldn't help overhearing what you were saying, Joanna. I'm sure you'll work something out with Ian, but Sophie will have to be very careful when it comes to choosing the right person to replace you.'

'Well, it's all a long way off,' Joanna said cheerfully. 'Lots of things can happen before then.'

'Such as?' Sophie asked curiously, and Joanna laughed.

'Your guess is as good as mine, but fate has a way of doing unexpected things.' She glanced at Helen, who nodded in agreement.

Sophie suddenly felt uncomfortable. It was almost as though Joanna and Helen were thinking along similar lines, and she longed to know what was in their minds. Was it, she wondered, that they were contemplating the eventual merger of the two practices? She knew that they both considered it a good solution to the difficulties existing at present, and this was disturbing. About to ask them outright, she was interrupted by the telephone, and, answering it, she was astonished to hear Robert's voice. He spoke as though there were no animosity whatever between them. Then, realising quickly that this must be a professional call, she waited calmly for an explanation. He said, 'I'm going to the zoo tomorrow morning. One or two problems and then a general inspection. You said you would like to come, so may I pick you up about eleven o'clock?'

She lost her breath for a moment. Their last meeting had ended so unpleasantly that it was difficult to change course suddenly.

'Well?' He sounded impatient and at last she found her voice.

'I—I—well, yes. I'd like to come, but. . .' She bit her lip, unable to remind him that they were hardly on speaking terms.

'But what? Are you booked up with operations?'

'No, it's not that. It was just. . .' Once more she stopped, and he gave a grim little laugh.

'Just that your personal feelings are stronger than your professional ones. Is that it?'

'I suppose it could be that.'

'Well, make up your mind, please. I have to tell Dawn that I don't need her help. As a matter of fact, I rarely do, but she has begun to take it for granted. It's one thing to take along another veterinary surgeon and quite another to be always accompanied by a nurse, however attractive. It gives rise to rather unwelcome banter from the staff.'

Sophie stiffened and was about to make a sharp retort, then she relaxed. 'All right. I'll come,' she said and put down the receiver to meet two pairs of eyes that looked so astonished that she burst out laughing.

'Which one was that?' Joanna demanded. 'Giles or Robert?'

'Why should you suppose it was either?' Sophie asked drily, then she added, 'It was a professional call. Robert had previously offered to show me round the zoo and explain the veterinary work he does there.' She paused. 'Naturally, although I don't like him personally, I do like the chance of widening my knowledge.' There was silence as they glanced at each other, and Sophie said irritably, 'It's exactly as I said. Purely professional.'

'If you say so.' Joanna looked unconvinced, but Helen said smoothly,

'I'm sure you're right. It's an opportunity you shouldn't miss.'

'The rest of the day passed uneventfully. Surgeries brought several more clients in, there was no more talk of Robert, and then it was time to get ready for Giles. Wearing a dress of soft blue wool which enhanced the startling beauty of her eyes, Sophie went to ask Joanna's opinion.

This was given with frank envy. 'You look lovely. You make me decide to go on a diet immediately, though even if I starved for a month I'd never get a waist as slim as yours.' She paused. 'You say you'll probably be bored, but I bet Giles won't.'

Sophie shrugged. 'I don't suppose it will be very exciting, but, as I said, it makes a break. I think Giles knows that I don't take him seriously.'

All the same, Giles looked handsome and very prosperous when he drove up in his luxurious car. The meal came well up to expectations and the wine he selected made the blood course through Sophie's veins. She refused the final glass he tried to press on her, but, even then, when they stepped outside the hotel the fresh, salty air caused her head to swim a little. He took her arm as she hesitated at the top of the steps and, as they walked along the deserted promenade, his arm slid round her.

'Just look at that moon shining on the water,' he said. 'I promised you a romantic walk — is this romantic enough?'

Sophie laughed. 'Don't get carried away, Giles. It's a lovely evening and this walk is just what I need to clear my head, but let's leave it at that.'

He stopped and pulled her into his arms. 'Sophie—you must know how I feel about you. Come on—relax and let me. . .' His lips were on hers before she could stop him. Held so tightly, she had to endure his demanding kiss for what seemed an eternity. Suddenly she heard the sound of an approaching car on the road running alongside the promenade, and as its headlights shone on them, she tried to pull away, turning her head so that his kisses fell on to the side of her face and down on to her shoulder. The car slowed down and a chill swept over as she caught a glimpse of the driver. For a few moments the headlights stayed, then she heard the noise of acceleration and once more all was quiet.

Lifting his head, Giles looked down on her stricken face.

He said slowly, 'Cold and indifferent—is that how you feel about me?'

She nodded and he winced. Then releasing her, he turned away. Looking out over the silvery water, she wondered whether it really was Robert who had been a spectator of what was apparently a passionate embrace. She might have been mistaken, of course, but no—she felt sure she was right. Of all the unfortunate things to happen. On the other hand, he might not have recognised her, might have thought some girl was in need of help, then decided they were two harmless lovers and driven away. That was far more likely.

Taking comfort from the thought, she drew a long breath and Giles turned.

'All right, Sophie. I can take a hint. Let's go back to the car.'

They sat in silence until he reached Broom House,

then he got out and went round to open the passenger door. As she began to thank him, he said drily, 'Bad judgment on my part. I thought—well, I won't bother you any more.'

There was no one about when she let herself into the house, and thankfully she went quietly up to her room. Sinking down on her bed, she tried to calm her thoughts. Then, with a shock, she remembered her promise to go to the zoo. For a moment or two she toyed with the idea of making some excuse in order to get out of what would be an embarrassing situation. No, that would be merely drawing attention to something that, after all, had nothing to do with him. He had probably come to the same conclusion and if she tried to give some kind of explanation he would raise his eyebrows and look at her in astonishment, and she would feel utterly foolish. For a moment his face rose before her—the deep, thoughtful eyes, the firm mouth—and suddenly she felt a surge of longing. If only it had been he instead of Giles who had kissed her in the moonlight. The fantasy lasted until suddenly she thrust it aside. The whole idea was crazy, the result of her fevered imagination. She would feel quite different in the morning.

But when morning came she still had to keep a firm hold on her feelings, especially when Joanna pressed her to describe her evening with Giles. She did her best to make light of it, describing in detail the dinner they had eaten, and only hesitated a little when it came to the stroll along the promenade. That, too, she managed to turn into a joke, while keeping back the unwelcome sighting of Robert. Finally she shrugged indifferently.

'Nothing to it, really. Just a pleasant evening out. What did you expect?'

Joanna grinned. 'Too much, obviously. My romantic mind must have been working overtime. Actually, I'm rather glad. I don't think Giles is the right man for you, in spite of all his future expectations.'

Relieved that she had not betrayed her real feelings, Sophie concentrated on the morning surgery, which, however, was not very busy. Helen came in towards the end, and, with no outside calls for her to go to, Joanna looked rather depressed. Picking up a copy of the *Veterinary Record*, she leafed through it, then suddenly exclaimed, 'It says here that there is an increase in Blue Ear Disease in pigs. Mr Jarvis won't like that.'

'"Blue Ear Disease" — what on earth is that?' Helen queried. 'It sounds frightful.'

'Well, it's a bit of a mystery.' Joanna put down her cup and proceeded to enlighten her. 'The symptoms are a low-grade fever, and the pig's extremities, especially the ears, turn blue. It causes abortions in sows and severe piglet mortality. It's highly contagious. It can be spread by wind over short distances.'

'Is there any treatment? Any particular drugs that you ought to acquire in readiness for an outbreak here?'

'No. There probably won't be a vaccine available for some years, so, as yet, there's no specific treatment. The only good thing about it is that it lasts for six months, then immunity is acquired.' She stopped at the sound of a car in the courtyard. Glancing out of the window, she said, 'Off you go, Sophie. Robert has arrived.'

He was holding the passenger door open for her, and his face gave nothing away. He greeted her calmly and as he turned the ignition key he said, 'I have to see to a young leopard and treat the hippo, who, they tell me, is a bit off colour. Then, if there's time, I'll do a general inspection.'

'That sounds interesting.' Sophie matched her tone to his. 'You must have some strange problems and strange ways in which to deal with them.'

'A lot of it is guesswork, of course. Wild animals tend to hide away when they fall ill or are injured, and those in captivity try to do the same, but it's almost impossible for them. Especially when lots of visitors are milling around as they will be today.' He stopped suddenly. 'Am I boring you? You seem rather faraway.'

'Of course I'm not bored. Your work at the zoo is so different from my usual day-to-day surgeries.'

'Does that mean that you're tired of small-animal work?'

'Goodness, no! I love it and there's always plenty of variety. But zoo work is an extension of my experience. I wouldn't miss it for worlds.'

He nodded. 'You're obviously a dedicated vet. What will you do when you're married to Giles Brandon? Give it all up?'

The astonishing question, asked in an ordinary conversational tone, made her gasp. She turned to stare at him and saw that he was smiling — a twisted smile that made her colour rise quickly. She said coldly, 'I suppose you ask that stupid question because you saw Giles and me on the promenade in Seabourne last night. Well, you've jumped to the wrong conclusion. People often do when they spy on others.'

'So you saw my car, did you? I was going to an urgent call — certainly not spying. But in full moonlight on a deserted promenade you did rather attract attention. I slowed down because for a moment I thought you might need help. Then I drew the obvious conclusion and drove off as quickly as possible.'

'What conclusion?' Sophie asked scornfully. 'Why should you suppose that a casual kiss means marriage?'

'Ah, well. It depends on what you mean by casual. It looked pretty serious to me. As for its meaning marriage...well, in fact I should think Giles is a pretty good catch for any girl—even a beautiful girl like you.'

'That,' said Sophie icily, 'is adding insult to injury.' She drew a long, furious breath. 'You can drop me at that bus-stop over there. Now, please. Slow down.'

He shook his head. 'No. We're going to the zoo, remember? Don't be childish.'

He merely accelerated and, as he passed the bus-stop, he laughed—a grim little laugh that filled Sophie with even more anger. She said no more, but her thoughts were bitter. How could she have had that fantasy about him last night? She must have been mad. It was probably the effect of the wine that Giles had plied her with so freely. The thought made her smile wryly, then she bit her lip as she caught a puzzled glance from Robert. He said, 'That's better. The situation has its funny side, after all. I must admit I was, as they say, "struck all of a heap" when I caught sight of you in Giles's arms.'

'I'm not smiling at that and I'm not interested in what you thought,' she snapped, then fell silent until they arrived at the zoo. As they got out of the car, she made a mental resolve that this would be the last visit she would make in Robert's company. Her veterinary interest must be sacrificed in order to avoid his taunting remarks.

Accompanied by the head keeper, they made their

way towards the leopards' enclosure. It was a large, grassy paddock, wired in over the top to stop the high-climbing cats from escaping. The keeper called, 'Sue, Sue — come here,' and a young leopard came up to the bars and rubbed herself against them while he stroked her back.

'I've known her since she was born,' he said. 'I remember picking her up and playing with her, but now, although she's friendly up to a point, she's gradually becoming more dangerous. It's a shame, really. It's a great feeling when a wild animal shows you affection, but even though she was born in captivity she'll always be a wild creature with the instincts of a killer.' He paused and turned to Robert. 'Look. . .' He pointed to the leopard's right cheek, where there was an ugly swelling oozing with pus. 'It's no better, as you can see.'

Robert frowned. 'It's certainly not healing with antibiotics in her drinking-water. I'll have to open it up. Have you got those bullets for the dart gun yet?'

'Due tomorrow,' said the keeper briefly.

'Well, I'll have to leave it till then. I must dart her with a long-acting anaesthetic. Then I'll drain it, cauterise it and pack it round with antibiotics. What do you think she weighs now? About ninety pounds?'

'Near enough,' said the keeper.

As they walked away, Robert turned to Sophie.

'My query about the weight is to ascertain the dose of anaesthetic to put in the barrel of the dart which is shot into the animal by the Cap Chur gun. One must have a fairly accurate idea of the patient's weight. It's not difficult with small creatures, but with the large ones it's possible to be a hundred pounds or so out, and an overdose could be dangerous for the animal.

VETS IN OPPOSITION

An underdose, of course, would be dangerous for the vet.'

'Where do you aim for?' Sophie asked, and the keeper answered,

'The dart has to go into the haunch, and that's important. Luckily Mr Sheldrake is a good shot. He has to avoid doing damage to parts of the body where there is no muscle. For instance, if the dart penetrated the abdomen the animal would die.'

'Now for our second problem,' Robert said. 'The hippo. You said he was off colour?'

'Yes, off his food. He hasn't passed anything for twenty-four hours. I think I know what's caused the trouble. We cleaned out his quarters a couple of days ago and put him outside while it was being done. There was a children's outing that day and I'm afraid it's the old story. Someone has probably thrown him some rubbish which he's swallowed.'

Sophie gazed at the huge, ugly monster with his great broad head and tiny protuding eyes. He was lying half submerged in his pool, and Robert, after looking at him closely, said, 'I've forgotten my rubber boots. I'll just nip back to my car and fetch them.'

The keeper laughed. 'Yes. Very necessary. He might bite your toes off if you go in barefoot.'

Returning, Robert opened his case and filled a jar with medicine. Then, wading in towards the hippo, he said soothingly, 'Poor old chap. Got a bit of indigestion, have you? Come on—open up.'

Bending down, he tickled the hippo under his chin, and, to Sophie's amusement, the great jaws opened. Quickly Robert threw the liquid in and the enormous mouth closed again.

'That's good,' the keeper said approvingly. 'It means

he's swallowed it. It's always a tricky job dosing a hippo. When he opens his mouth, a valve closes to prevent him swallowing when he's underwater, and he could have ejected that medicine if he had wanted to.'

Suddenly, to Sophie's alarm, she saw the hippo's mouth open again and his jaws close round Robert's boot. She watched nervously as he bent down and pushed gently at the huge mouth, and gradually, reluctantly, he was released. He walked out of the pool, grinning broadly.

'I've met that before with hippos,' he said. 'They seem to like the taste of rubber. They don't mean any harm.' He glanced at his watch. 'General inspection now?'

The keeper nodded. 'If you like, but it will have to be on your own this morning. I've got a meeting with the management.'

'Right,' Robert said. 'If I see anything wrong, I'll ring you later from my surgery.' He turned to Sophie. 'Let's have a coffee first, shall we?'

The keeper turned back. 'No need for you to go into the restaurant. It's crowded out with school kids. I'll get coffee sent into my office. You can be on your own there.'

Sophie frowned to herself. She would have preferred the noise and distraction of the public restaurant to sitting quietly in a room alone with Robert, but it was impossible to refuse. Robert, glancing at her for confirmation, saw her frown, but ignored it and nodded his thanks to the keeper.

A few minutes later, installed in the office, a small room looking out on to the quarantine quarters, Sophie tried to find a topic of conversation that would keep things on a professional basis. Stirring her coffee, she asked, 'How is the spot-nosed monkey?'

Robert smiled. 'He's doing fine. There are two girl keepers who spend as much time as they can with him and are giving him so many titbits that he's getting thoroughly spoiled. But when he sees me he gets very angry and chatters away furiously. Won't let me touch him. Obviously blames me for sticking a needle into him, and I expect he always will.'

That seemed to be the end of that topic, so Sophie tried something else. 'These quarantine quarters — what have they got in there?'

'At the moment, not much. Four Barbary apes. And that reminds me — I have to do my visit there tomorrow. I report on them every week for the Ministry of Agriculture.'

'What do you look for? Rabies?'

'Yes, mainly. I look for listlessness, restlessness — anything abnormal. The regulations are very strict.'

This led to a discussion on the EC wishing to abolish quarantine altogether, and Robert grew heated as he spoke of the risks. Then there was a long pause during which Sophie drank her coffee and avoided looking at her companion. Suddenly he said, 'Would you mind putting off a general inspection of the animals till tomorrow? I have to come then to do the quarantine report and also I must dart and treat that leopard. I'm sure you would like to see how that works. Afterwards we could look round at leisure.'

'Well, yes, perhaps it would be better,' Sophie said, but made a mental note to refuse all further invitations. It would be a professional sacrifice, but these outings with Robert must stop. It was getting impossible to keep their relationship in two separate compartments.

Her feelings about him were so mixed, and Dawn's warning echoed constantly in her mind. He was not to be trusted. Then her heart gave a little lurch as she met his eyes. There was a sad expression in them, as though he could read her thoughts and wanted to convince her that she was mistaken. Impulsively she asked, 'Why are you looking at me like that?' and immediately regretted having spoken her thoughts aloud. She tried to cover it up with a laugh. 'What I mean is, are you worried about getting back? If so, we'd better go now, hadn't we?'

He shook his head. 'No rush. You ask if I'm worried — well, yes, I am. Shall I tell you why?'

She hesitated. 'I don't — I mean — I don't want to know anything if it's not professional.'

He gazed at her in silence, then he said, 'Well, in a way, it is professional. It concerns our future. I would very much like to know if you are contemplating marrying Giles, in spite of your apparent denial. No need to stiffen up like that — you must see that it would affect me professionally.'

Her mouth was dry and she wished she hadn't finished her coffee. She moistened her lips, then said, 'I can't see that it should matter to you.'

'It has a lot to do with me. For two reasons in particular. I'll give you the least important one first. If you marry Giles your life will be quite different. You certainly won't have time to practise as a vet down here. You will have to live in London until he inherits his uncle's estate. Then you'll be the lady of the manor, so to speak.' His tone had become cynical and mocking as he went on, 'Now I don't suppose Joanna will want to continue working here if you leave. She and Ian have other plans. So I would like to buy your practice —

have first refusal, in any case.' He paused. 'The other reason is not professional, so I won't go into that. Not until I know whether or not you are going to marry Giles.'

Concentrating on his first reason, Sophie did not give much attention to his last remark. She thought, At least he's quite open about wanting my practice. But he's forgotten one thing. She said, 'I don't think you realise that you couldn't possibly buy it. My godmother would certainly not want strangers on her property.' Then another thought struck her and she added mockingly, 'Why do you talk of buying? My practice isn't worth anything yet. You know all this, so why are you talking such nonsense?'

He looked at her with a strange expression in his eyes.

'The reason for that is linked up with my second one. Do you want to hear it?'

She stared at him, then looked quickly away. His gaze was so disturbing that she felt herself trembling. Why did this hateful man arouse her emotions in this way? Shaking off her confusion, she said scornfully, 'Another trumped-up story, I suppose.'

He said evenly, 'My chief reason is wanting to know if you and Giles——'

'Will you stop harping on that?' She was suddenly furious. 'He's nothing to me and I'm sick of you prying into my personal life.'

His gaze became even more penetrating. He drummed with his fingers on the table for a few moments then he said, 'So the field is still open, is it?'

'What on earth do you mean by that?' She stared at him in bewilderment, and he smiled.

'What I said.' Getting up from the table, he added,

'We'd better go. I suppose you wouldn't like to have a quick lunch with me? Not here, of course, but somewhere on the way back.'

'No, thank you,' she said coldly. 'I'd like to go straight back to my surgery.'

'Right. Well, will you come tomorrow, then? Shall I pick you up at the same time as I did this morning?'

She spoke with great deliberation. 'I've decided not to come any more. It's been very interesting, but I don't want to continue going round with you. People tend to get hold of wrong ideas, just as you did last night.'

His eyes darkened as he looked down at her. 'Very well, if that's how you feel.'

He held the door open and as she passed through he said something under his breath and touched her very lightly on the shoulder — a caressing kind of touch that caused her to give an involuntary shiver. He frowned, began to say something, then stopped. Shutting the door behind them, he followed her to his car.

CHAPTER EIGHT

FOR three days there was no communication between the two practices. At Broom House the small-animal work was steadily increasing, but progress with regard to farm work was very slow. Discussing the situation after morning surgery, Joanna, Helen and Sophie tried to come to terms with the way things were working out. Then Joanna asked thoughtfully, 'Sophie, when you first made up your mind to set up on your own, did you contemplate doing any large-animal work at all?'

Sophie frowned, trying to recall just how she had felt while she was gathering information from the lecturers at the veterinary congress. At last she said slowly, 'Well, having done nothing but small-animal work for two years in London, I have to say that apart perhaps from the odd pony I never really considered anything else. My dream was to build up a prosperous small-animal practice and later on take on an assistant.' She paused as she saw the wry expression on Joanna's face. 'Don't look so woebegone, Joanna. When I saw you, I knew you were the ideal person to share with, and I've never regretted it.'

'Hmm. That's all very well. But you didn't reckon on my being so keen on farm work, did you?'

'No. But it's an asset. It's only because we've had the bad luck to find ourselves in competition with Robert and Ian, otherwise we could have had all their present clients.'

'I'm not so sure of that,' Joanna said pensively.

'From what I can make out, most mixed practices employ male vets for the large animals.' She frowned. 'You can't get away from the fact that women vets aren't looked on kindly by farmers. They don't think it's what they call "right" for women to do jobs like castrations, and it seems to embarrass the poor dears to talk of putting heifers to the bull and dealing with calving cases, or to discuss the sexual behaviour of their animals.'

Helen said quietly, 'That's exactly what Edward was saying the other day. But I can't see that it matters very much. You're both very good at small-animal work and that is certainly building up very well. Any farm work that does come in can be a sort of bonus.'

'Eminently sensible as usual.' Sophie smiled at her godmother, then, turning to Joanna, she said, 'The point is that I feel you're disappointed. Am I right?'

Joanna shrugged. 'Perhaps, but I think it would be more apt to say that I'm disillusioned. Not,' she added hastily, 'with being here. It's lovely and friendly and so comfortable. What I mean is that I've finally been forced to admit that the large-animal side of veterinary practice is still controlled by men. I always knew it, of course, but I hoped it would change. Now I don't think it ever will. That's what depresses me. It also makes me wonder if I'm not a drag on you, Sophie. The farming bills don't amount to much as the ones who do call me in always think they're doing me a favour and consequently shouldn't be charged much. So the time I spend with them would be more profitably employed here in the surgery.'

'You're talking rubbish,' Sophie laughed. 'I bet you've been discussing it with Ian, who, nice as he is, is a male vet, and they're like the farmers. You've got to prove them wrong.'

Helen, who was standing by the window, said suddenly, 'Here's another client coming up the drive — I think that's Mr Jarvis's car.'

It was indeed, and he came into the surgery carrying a bundle wrapped in a towel. Placing it on the table, he said ruefully, 'I seem fated to come across casualties. This is a dog I found in the road. Obviously hit by a vehicle and just left to die.' He lifted the towel. 'It's not dead yet, but it's in a bad way. A collar on, but no name or address.'

Sophie looked down at the unconscious West Highland terrier and saw that his breathing was rapid and shallow. There was a little blood around his mouth and his eyes were badly bruised. Putting on her stethoscope, she sounded his heart very carefully, then lifted his lips and looked at his gums. Joanna, standing beside her, said, 'I'll get the heart stimulant and you'll want to give an injection of blood coagulant, won't you?'

Sophie nodded. 'Yes. I'm pretty sure there's internal bleeding — his gums are very pale. We'd better fix up a drip to replace the blood that's leaking into his body.'

Joanna handed her the two syringes, then began fixing up the drip. Putting a length of rubber tubing on to the attachment, she turned a bottle upside-down to allow the liquid to flow. Then Sophie pinched the end of the tube, put a needle into the dog's vein, and joined it to the tube. She stuck a piece of adhesive tape round it to stop the needle from coming out and hung the bottle on to a hook just over the dog. Standing back, she watched the bubbles coming up into the bottle. A few minutes later she listened again to the heart and once more studied the gums. They were paler than ever, almost white, and she shook her head slowly.

'His breathing is growing feebler,' she said. 'I think his liver may have been crushed. I can give him two more injections in about half an hour, but—' she shook her head again'—it's a losing battle, I'm afraid.'

Mr Jarvis pulled on his cap. 'I have to go, so I must leave him in your hands. I don't know where he comes from, though I think I've seen him around occasionally.'

When he had gone they stood in silence, watching keenly, but without much hope. Joanna said thoughtfully, 'I've seen that dog before somewhere. Mind you, "Westies" all look rather alike, so I might be wrong. . . Oh, dear, I hope I am.' She paused. 'I think—I think it belongs to Dawn.'

'Dawn? Oh, God!' Sophie looked aghast and for a moment they stared at each other. Then Sophie turned to Helen. 'Would you ring Sheldrake's surgery and ask if her dog is missing?'

While they waited the two girls concentrated on their patient. His breathing was slowing down. There was a long pause, one more breath, and that was all. Sophie heaved a long sigh, then looked up as Helen came back to the table, her face drawn and anxious.

'I spoke to Robert—he called Dawn and she became so hysterical that I couldn't understand her. Robert spoke again and said they'd be right over.'

Sophie passed her hand over her forehead, then began to unfasten the drip. Looking down at the pathetic little body lying so still on the table, she said, 'I'd better leave him like this for Dawn to see. We've done all that was possible, so she can't blame us.'

A few minutes later, Dawn rushed up to the table,

followed closely by Robert. Rejecting his comforting arm, she turned to glare at Sophie.

'Why didn't you call me sooner? Why didn't you ask Robert to fetch him?' She burst into tears. 'I'm sure he could have saved him with all the modern equipment we have. Why. . .?' She sobbed loudly, and Robert put his hand on her shoulder.

His voice was full of sympathy. 'I know it's hard to accept, Dawn, but all that could have been done has been done. There was internal bleeding that couldn't be stopped even with the drip and the injections Sophie must have given.'

'Ah, but did she?' Dawn looked at him wildly. 'How do you know she didn't just let him die, knowing he belonged to me?'

'That's a terrible thing to say.' Robert was clearly horrified. He turned to Sophie. 'You'll have to forgive her. She's in a state of shock.'

'So are we.' Joanna's face was as white as Sophie's, who stood motionless and speechless as Dawn's words echoed in her ears. 'To accuse us of letting the dog die—that's plain wicked!'

'She doesn't really mean it,' Robert defended Dawn reluctantly.

'Oh, yes, I do.' Dawn's eyes filled with hatred as she glared at Sophie, and she was about to say more when Helen said quietly, 'Come into the office. I'll make some tea—it will help you. We're all terribly sorry, but your dog was dying when he was brought in.'

'What do you know about it?' Dawn muttered rudely, and Robert tightened his grip on her shoulder.

'Come along. You need that tea.'

Sophie watched as he led her into the office and Joanna picked up a chair.

'There are only two in there,' she said, and Sophie picked up another one. Then she stopped.

'What would she like to do with her dog? Will you ask her or shall I?'

'I think I'd better be the one,' Joanna said, then Robert came out to pick up the remaining chair. He turned to Sophie.

'I can't apologise enough for Dawn. I don't think she really knew what she was saying.'

'I hope she didn't,' Sophie said bitterly, 'but I'm afraid she did.'

'Oh, come, now. The poor girl was distraught.'

'So am I.' Sophie's mouth quivered. 'It's bad enough losing the dog—you must know how it affects a vet—but to be accused of practically killing it out of spite...' She swallowed hard. 'I'm sorry. I'll feel better in a minute, but I just can't imagine why she dislikes me so.'

Joanna said shortly, 'She's jealous of you. That's why.'

'Jealous? That's ridiculous. Why should she be?'

Joanna glanced at Robert, saw his mouth tighten, then said quietly, 'If you can't guess, then it's not up to me to tell you.'

Sophie began to speak, but at that moment Helen came out of the office.

'Isn't that kettle boiling yet? Dawn is weeping. Robert, hadn't you better go and see if you can comfort her?'

Joanna looked scornful. 'Yes. That's what she wants, obviously.'

Sophie drew in her breath. 'For goodness' sake, stop talking about her like that.' She turned to Robert. 'Will you take the dog back with you or shall I keep it here for a while?'

He said, 'Keep it here for a while. As soon as she's had her tea, I'll take her back. I'll come for the dog later on.'

She nodded, then, as he picked up another chair, she said, 'Leave that one, please. I'll have my tea in here.'

He put it down, then, unexpectedly, he put his hand on her shoulder. 'Poor Sophie. Don't take it too hard. I know just how you must feel.' Bending down, he kissed her gently on the cheek, leaving her staring after him. Then, turning, she saw Joanna nodding her head, as though pleased at the sight. The next moment Helen came in again, quickly made the tea, poured some out for Sophie, and said quietly, 'I'll get rid of Dawn as soon as I can. Drink this in the dispensary, then she won't see you when Robert takes her away.'

Seated behind the wooden partition, Sophie thought about Robert's kiss. It meant nothing, she told herself; he'll probably do the same to Dawn. A picture rose in her mind of Dawn enfolded in his arms when they were alone in his surgery, and it tormented her so much that she got up hurriedly and put the little dog in a cage to await Robert's collection. Back in the dispensary, she stayed until she heard the office door open. They went out quietly and she gave a long sigh of relief.

Helen and Joanna came out looking very serious, and Joanna said, 'Robert tried to shut Dawn up, but she's evidently going to make trouble for us. She's being very vindictive.'

Sophie's heart sank, but she braced herself.

'I've come up against her sort before. When I was working in London, we often got clients who blamed us if their pets died. Sometimes they complained to the Veterinary Council, but as we were innocent we were quite rightly vindicated.'

Joanna shrugged gloomily. 'She said something about telling the local newspaper.'

'Nonsense,' Helen said firmly. 'You heard what Robert said.' She looked at Sophie's stricken face and added, 'He told her that if she gave them some garbled story he would sack her on the spot. He would too — he was so angry at her threat that I'm sure she would never dare to carry it out.'

Joanna cheered up. 'That's true. I don't think we need to worry with him to defend us.'

'We don't need his protection,' Sophie said sharply. 'We've nothing to reproach ourselves for.' She was silent for a moment then she said, 'Look, Joanna — when he calls to collect the dog I don't want to see him. So would you mind staying here in the surgery until he comes in? I'm going to disappear until he's gone.'

Joanna raised her eyebrows. 'What's he done wrong?'

'I just don't want to see him, that's all. As far as I'm concerned, the incident is over and I don't want him meddling in our affairs.'

She turned towards the door, but stopped as the telephone rang and Joanna picked it up. Listening for a moment, she put her hand over the mouthpiece. 'It's Mr Jarvis.' Turning back, she said, 'Yes, of course. I'll come right away. Yes, I'm afraid the dog died.' Replacing the instrument, she said, 'Sorry Sophie. I have to go. One of his sows is off colour. I don't suppose it's serious, but he's so terrified of Blue Ear Disease that he watches them like a hawk.'

'If you want to disappear, Sophie,' Helen said, 'I'll hold the fort, though quite frankly I don't understand why you want to avoid Robert. He's been most sympathetic about the whole thing.'

Sophie flushed, sensing the disapproval in her godmother's voice. Wondering if she was really rather stupid, she searched her mind and acknowledged the truth. It was his attitude towards Dawn, treating her with such compassion and even apologising for her. She looked up and met Helen's understanding smile.

'Don't worry.' Her godmother's voice held a hint of amusement. 'It's natural to feel jealous. I'm sure everything will work out for the best.'

Sophie blinked, startled at the way in which Helen had read her thoughts. Before she had time to find a suitable reply, the telephone rang again.

'Could I bring my dog in for his booster injection, please? I have to put him into kennels tomorrow as I have to go away for some time and they insist that he be fully vaccinated.'

Telling the caller to come right away, Sophie reflected wryly that fate was against her, and when Helen decided that she wasn't needed in the surgery it seemed that she was destined to face Robert alone.

He came in when Sophie was giving her booster injection to her client's dog, and as soon as she had finished with them he confronted her.

'Don't look so stricken,' he said. 'I've calmed Dawn down. There'll be no more trouble.'

As if it were the most natural thing in the world, he put his arms round her and held her close. For a moment she relaxed against him, then as his words penetrated she saw a mental picture of those same arms encircling Dawn. She drew back.

'I'm not worrying, but I'm still shocked by Dawn's accusations—as a veterinary nurse she should know better.'

He shook his head. 'She's not a qualified nurse. I've trained her, but she hasn't gone in for the exams. Personally, I think she'd do better in another career.'

Releasing herself from his arms, Sophie said drily, 'The career Dawn wants is that of a veterinary surgeon's wife.' She gave him a cold smile and turned away, but he took a step forward and gripped her shoulders.

'What on earth are you talking about?'

She bit her lip, wondering if she had gone too far, then she said curtly, 'Work it out for yourself.'

For a minute there was silence, then he said softly, 'I can see what you're driving at, but you're quite wrong if you think there's anything between us. Perhaps this will convince you...'

Before she realised it, she was in his arms again, and this time he kissed her fiercely, a long kiss that left her feeling faint and breathless, and caused her heart to beat so fast that she felt sure he must be conscious of its wild throbbing. At last he lifted his head and his arms dropped to his sides. The expression on his face was so grim that it almost frightened her, and she stared at him speechlessly. Then her anger rose—anger at being treated so ruthlessly, as though he had the right to kiss her as and when he chose. Under his searching gaze she turned her back on him, and began to walk away, though her legs felt weak and shaky.

He said sharply, 'Wait. We must talk.'

It was a command that made her even more resentful.

'No,' she said icily. 'I've nothing to say to you. Take the dog and get out of my surgery.'

She went into the office and slammed the door behind her. A short time later she heard him drive away. Then, with a strange feeling of loss, depression swept over her. It was all too complicated. She knew now that she loved him, yet, at times, she seemed to hate him. She longed for the thrill of being in his arms, but she didn't trust him, and Dawn's words of warning still echoed in her mind. She sighed heavily. The only thing to do was to hold her emotions in check and get on with her work.

Twenty minutes later, she was still trying to forget the way he had looked at her before slamming the door behind him. It was a look so burning and intense that it had left her fearful and uncertain, and it was only by immersing herself in paperwork that she had been able to recapture some of her habitual calm. Then suddenly she heard a car sweep into the yard, and, getting up from her desk, she felt her heart leap uncomfortably once more as she saw Robert getting out of his Land Rover. For a wild moment she contemplated locking the door against him, then, pulling herself together, she prepared to face him.

To her astonishment he was smiling as he said, 'No need to look so unwelcoming. I've come to see you under another guise. I'm the friend who shares a mutual interest. I've just heard about a very good antique shop opening over at Warmly. How about taking an afternoon off next week and driving over with me to have a look round? We could combine it with a snack lunch on the way.' He stopped and laughed. 'Oh, Sophie — if you could throw your caution to the winds. It will do you good, help you to get over the bad time you've just had.'

She fought the temptation with all her strength, and opened her mouth to refuse, but no words came out. Then she met his eyes and resistance collapsed. She said slowly, 'I ought to say no, but I'm going to say yes. On one condition.'

He smiled ruefully, 'I think I can guess. Friendship— nothing more. Is that it?'

She nodded and flushed as she saw his eyes darken.

'OK. If that's the only way I can persuade you. How about Tuesday?'

She pondered. 'Tuesday? Yes, maybe. But you understand that anything could happen to change it.'

'Of course. One of the hazards of being a vet. But, all being well, I'll keep Tuesday free from midday onwards.' He gave her a long look, smiled, and went out to his car.

She stood still for several minutes, wondering what was happening to her. Was she losing control of a difficult situation? Well, perhaps on Tuesday she would find out more about Robert's wish for friendship.

Sitting over sandwiches and coffee later that day, Joanna asked suddenly, 'Are you all right, Sophie? You look awfully peaky and you've hardly eaten a thing. Is anything wrong?'

'No.' Sophie forced a smile. 'On the contrary. I was just thinking that we're doing rather well with one or two steady accounts.'

'I suppose we are. But, apart from Mr Jarvis, the few farmers I've done work for haven't paid their bills yet.'

Sophie shrugged. 'They often take a long time. That's what I've heard, anyway.'

'They're still very patronising to me, keep hinting that they're doing me a favour.' She sighed, 'Men!'

'I'm sure that doesn't include Ian.' Helen sounded amused as she came into the room. 'I hope I'm not interrupting a feminist discussion, but I want to ask you something. Will you both come to a little party I'm planning for next week? A small return for Edward's hospitality. Nothing like as grand, of course.'

Joanna pulled out a chair for her. 'Just what we need to cheer ourselves up. May we help you with the preparations?'

'Betty is very good at doing all the bits and pieces. She loves it. I'm not allowed to lift a finger. By the way——' Helen paused, '—she has been gathering some gossip that will probably interest you. Apparently Dawn——'

'I never want to hear that name again,' Sophie broke in, then felt rather foolish as Helen raised her eyebrows.

'Don't be silly. I'm not going to keep this to myself, so you'll have to listen. You don't mind, do you, Joanna?'

'Not at all. I'm all for a bit of gossip. You mustn't take any notice of Sophie. She's still sore about Dawn's accusations when her dog died.'

'Yes, well, that was very bad. Still, it appears that she's quietened down considerably. The gossip is that she is thinking of resigning from the practice and going back to her home town. The surgery cleaner—it was she who told Betty—says Robert doesn't seem to mind, though it will probably be very inconvenient to lose his veterinary nurse.'

Joanna said cynically, 'I expect she's putting on an act just to——'

'For goodness' sake!' Sophie interrupted irritably. 'Let's talk about something less boring.' She bit her lip as she saw a quick glance pass between Joanna and Helen. Did they guess why she was so short-tempered of late? Did they suspect how mixed-up she was in her feelings for Robert? Suddenly, to her relief, the telephone rang, Joanna picked it up, wrote down the message, and came back to the table, looking elated.

'That was Mr Sugden over at Hill Farm. I've only been there once and I thought he didn't like me much, but now he wants me to do a dozen PDs tomorrow.'

'What exactly are PDs?' Helen asked, and Joanna said,

'Pregnancy diagnoses.' She turned to Sophie. 'I have to be there by nine o'clock, so I won't be able to help with the morning surgery.'

But the surgery on Monday morning was not as busy as it had been of late. Helen said consolingly, 'It's because it's such a wet day. People don't come out unless it's absolutely necessary.'

Sophie agreed and looked out of the window. 'It's fairly bucketing down. It's nearly ten o'clock, so let's have coffee, shall we?'

They were waiting for the kettle to boil when the telephone rang again and Helen picked it up.

She gave a horrified gasp as she listened, then turned to Sophie.

'It's Hill Farm. Joanna has had an accident. A cow lashed out at her and she slipped on the wet floor. Her leg may be broken. She's been taken to the Seabourne General Hospital.' She turned back to the telephone. 'Thank you for telling us. We'll go there right away.'

Sophie stood white-faced and trembling. 'Oh, poor

Joanna. What awful bad luck.' She got up hurriedly, spilling her coffee and looking distraught, but Helen, ever practical, said,

'You'd better gather some of her things together — you know, night clothes, dressing-gown, toilet articles et cetera — while I get my car out. I'll drive you in. You look too shaken up to drive well.'

CHAPTER NINE

To SOPHIE's and Helen's surprise, Ian Woodall, looking anxious and drawn, was waiting for them at the hospital.

'Joanna asked the farmer to ring me before they took her away in the ambulance. I've seen her for a few minutes, but now they've taken her to be X-rayed. I'm pretty certain her leg is broken, but how badly remains to be seen.' At the sight of Sophie's distress, he relaxed a little and added, 'Let's go and get some tea while we're waiting.'

They sat quietly for a while, then Ian said, 'Joanna was terribly worried about her work, but I think I've managed to reassure her. I told her that I would do her large-animal work for her. . .' He glanced at Sophie. 'With your permission, of course.'

She was so preoccupied that she merely nodded, but she looked up sharply when he added, 'Dawn has offered to help with any difficult operations where you might need assistance.'

'Dawn?' Sophie shook her head fiercely. 'Oh, no. I don't want her near me.'

Ian frowned. 'She has her good points, Sophie. We're all sorry for Joanna and we appreciate how difficult it will be for you.'

'Well, I draw the line at Dawn,' Sophie said firmly, then, as she caught a reproachful look from Helen, she realised how ungenerous she sounded. She drew a long breath. 'I'm sorry. I shouldn't have said that. Thank

Dawn for her offer, please, and tell her I'll certainly call on her if necessary.'

Ian looked relieved. 'In an emergency like this, we must help each other out. It's better than getting a locum in — they cost the earth and sometimes do more harm than good. Not that Joanna was like that when she did a locum in the practice where we met. Actually she's very good at farm work. Mind you——' he gazed thoughtfully into his cup ' — I don't think it's easy for a girl. Anyhow, when we're married. . .' He stopped and looked at them self-consciously. 'Well, that's in the future.' He glanced at his watch. 'She should be back from X-Ray by now. I'll go and make some enquiries.'

Sophie smiled wryly as she watched his receding figure.

'Joanna will have her work cut out to convince him that she's the equal of any man when they set up in practice together.'

Helen laughed gently. 'I'll back Joanna when it comes to doing the work she likes. All the same——' she paused ' — this accident may change her attitude — who knows?'

'That accident could have happened to anyone — male or female,' Sophie said, 'and all vets have to face up to a certain amount of danger.' She got up as she saw Ian beckoning from the doorway. 'Oh, good. We're going to be able to see her.'

'She's in the surgical ward,' Ian said. 'The sister has allowed us ten minutes.'

As soon as they approached her bed, Joanna greeted them with a mixture of tears and rueful self-reproach.

'It was partly my own fault. I just wasn't quick enough when the wretched cow lashed out, and that wet floor. . .' She looked at Sophie apologetically. 'I'm terribly sorry to have messed things up like this.'

'Don't worry.' Sophie smiled reassuringly. 'Ian has got it all arranged. Everything will be OK—he's been very helpful.'

'Well, actually it was Robert who made the arrangements.' Ian turned to Sophie. 'He's coming to see you this evening to talk things over.'

'There's no need——' Sophie began, but once more the look in Helen's eyes checked her. 'Well, perhaps we'd better know how we stand.' She paused and looked at her friend affectionately. 'All you've got to do, Joanna, is to get that leg put right. By the way, what was the result of the X-ray?'

'A simple fracture. Nothing complicated,' Joanna said cheerfully. 'Once it's in plaster I'll be back. Perhaps tomorrow.'

'What? Surely not as soon as that,' Helen exclaimed. 'You're not to think of it, my dear.'

'Oh, yes. I'll be stomping round the surgery in no time. It isn't as though my arm is broken. No reason why I shouldn't do some of the simple work.'

Helen still looked doubtful, then she said tactfully, 'Sophie, I think we should leave Ian and Joanna alone for the few minutes that remain, don't you?'

Bending down, Sophie kissed her friend and wished her good luck, then, once outside the ward, she turned to her godmother.

'Will you come in and stay with me when Robert comes round?'

'Now why on earth should I do that? Surely you don't want a chaperone? If so, you must be about a hundred years out of date.' Helen shook her head reproachfully, then added, 'Actually, I can't if Robert comes in the evening. Edward is coming for a drink.'

Sophie flushed. Maybe her request sounded foolish, but the prospect of facing Robert after everything that had happened between them was disturbing. Then she pulled herself together. Obviously it was necessary to talk over arrangements, though it seemed to her that the offers of help were a little excessive. With Helen to assist her and Ian doing the farm work she was no worse off than if she had, as originally planned, set up in practice on her own. She would tell Robert that and let him know that she didn't need to be treated as though she were completely helpless.

He came round just as evening surgery was nearing its end.

Her last patient was an old Labrador bitch and it was quite obvious that an urgent operation was called for. Robert came forward and listened intently as the owners — a middle-aged man with an anxious-looking wife — asked nervously, 'You say there's a certain amount of risk. How much?'

Sophie frowned. 'There's always a risk in an operation like this when the bitch is elderly, but she can't go on — it's now become urgent.'

The man said, 'She's ten years old. Will the operation prolong her life for — say — two or three more years?'

Sophie hesitated. 'That's a difficult question. At her age, anything could happen, but this condition, once it's operated on, shouldn't cause any more problems.'

Husband and wife looked at each other, then the wife said, 'Our daughter is handicapped. She's in a wheelchair. We think she could probably be able to stand Sandy's loss a bit better in, say, a couple of years' time. She is the same age as Sandy—ten years old—and absolutely devoted to her.'

Sophie felt a sudden throb of anxiety, but she said cheerfully, 'I'll do my level best for her. I had to tell you about the risk, but I've done this operation on bitches who were older than Sandy, and they were all successful.'

Last instructions given, and the operation arranged for the following day, the couple went away, and Robert said, 'It's a pity, isn't it? About tomorrow, I mean. Tuesday—the day we fixed for our outing together.'

Sophie looked blank for a moment. 'Tuesday? Oh, yes, it's unfortunate, but——' she shrugged '—it doesn't seem important now in view of Joanna's accident.'

'Well, it was important to me.' He paused. 'We must fix another time when all this is over.' He paused again.

'Who is going to help you tomorrow?'

'Helen, I expect,' Sophie said coolly.

'Is she quite up to it? I would have thought that when there is a risk attached you would need someone who is used to helping in a crisis.'

'Helen has been adequate up till now, though she hasn't actually seen this operation. Joanna usually. . .' Sophie stopped, unwilling to betray the sudden fear that was clutching at her heart.

'What's the matter? You've gone pale. What's wrong?'

She tried to pull herself together, but it was impossible. Her voice trembled. 'Suddenly I've lost my nerve. Dawn's dog dying, now this Labrador who means so much to a handicapped child. Suppose. . .' Her voice faded and she felt bitterly ashamed as she tried to control her rising panic. She sat down, staring ahead, oblivious to Robert's presence. Suddenly she felt his arm round her.

'It's a natural reaction, but I'm not going to offer to do the operation for you. You must do it yourself or you'll never regain your confidence. I'll act as your nurse. I won't give advice, but if an emergency occurs I'll be able to help. How's that?'

She said nothing, then he added, 'Perhaps you'd rather have Dawn. She's very competent.'

Sophie came to life abruptly. 'Dawn? To help me recover my confidence? You must be crazy. It's because of her. . .' She stopped, 'I'll manage with Helen.'

He said firmly. 'Nevertheless I shall come and be in the background.'

With that he went away, leaving Sophie irritated by what she considered his dictatorial manner. It was bad enough that she should have to accept Ian's help with farm work, but that was necessary, if only to keep Joanna happy. She must, she resolved, keep Robert at a distance.

Next morning Helen set off early to see Joanna while Sophie dealt with several clients who, having heard of Joanna's accident, were sympathetic and concerned. It was surprising, she thought, how well the local people seemed to have accepted Joanna and herself, considering the short time they had been there. Perhaps it was the universal bond between animal lovers and vets that made it so easy to become part of the community. When the last client had gone Sophie looked at the time. The Labrador was not due in till later in the morning as the owners couldn't make it any earlier. Once more she felt her nerves quivering with apprehension, but when Helen came in she managed to hide her fears. The news of Joanna was good and, listening to the description of her cheerfulness, Sophie felt her own courage returning. But Helen was worried.

'Joanna is determined to come home today. She'll discharge herself if necessary. I'm sure she ought not to, but you know Joanna. She just wouldn't listen to me.'

Sophie frowned momentarily, then she said, 'You mustn't worry. Joanna's no fool. She won't do anything stupid. She won't come out of hospital if she doesn't feel strong enough.'

Helen shrugged. 'Perhaps you're right. Now, is there anything to do here?'

Reluctantly Sophie told her of Robert's imminent arrival, and Helen looked pleased. As she went out of the door, she turned. 'Mind you're nice to him,' she said.

But to Sophie's intense mortification it was Dawn who arrived and said calmly, 'Robert has been called out to a difficult calving case and I've been told to give you his apologies. Ian is going to the hospital, so I'm afraid you'll have to put up with me.' She hesitated. 'I know you're not pleased, but I thought it would be a good opportunity to say I'm sorry. I was suffering from shock at losing Snowy. I ought never to have accused you of letting him die. I'm really very, very sorry.'

Her face was pale and her voice was as cool as ever, but there was sincerity in her eyes, and Sophie drew a long breath and put out her hand.

'Let's forget it,' she said, and there was a long pause. Then, pointing to the Labrador, who had already arrived, Sophie said, 'She's ten years old and the pet of a handicapped child.' She stopped, then said slowly,

'Losing your dog has shaken me up so much that I'm very nervous about this case. Do you understand?'

Dawn's expression softened. 'Of course I do. I'd feel the same. But I'm sure that once you begin to operate all your professional training will take over.'

Administering the anaesthetic was Sophie's worst moment, but all went well. Then, with Dawn keeping careful watch on Sandy's breathing, Sophie took up a scalpel, and, after one long moment of hesitation, she made the first incision. Almost immediately her skill as a surgeon took over as Dawn had said it would. With full confidence she worked steadily and competently. Unpleasant and smelly as the operation was, she felt a surge of exultation when she cut the thread of the last suture and surveyed her unconscious patient. Dawn handed her a syringe filled with heart stimulant and soon Sandy was settled down in a warm recovery cage.

With a long sigh of relief, Sophie said, 'I'll just ring the owners and tell them that, so far, everything has gone well. Then we'll have a well deserved coffee.'

When Dawn had cleared up they sat down and relaxed. Then unexpectedly Dawn began to talk about herself.

At first Sophie listened with only mild interest as the other girl spoke of her involvement in veterinary work, which had begun when she had worked as a receptionist in a large practice in Shropshire, where Robert had been senior assistant. Then, at the sound of his name, Sophie stiffened, reluctantly fascinated as Dawn continued.

'I fell for him at once and he seemed attracted to me, but that was all there was to it for a long time. Unfortunately, just as we were on the verge of starting an affair, he heard that I had other irons in the fire.'

She shrugged. 'Well, I had to keep my options open, and there was someone else with whom I was involved. I was prepared to drop him, but Robert dropped me first.' She smiled bitterly. 'Like a hot brick. He's very intolerant, you know.' She stopped for a moment and eyed Sophie thoughtfully. 'Anyway, we remained friends, and when he decided to come down here and start his practice I asked if he would take me on as a pupil veterinary nurse. He agreed and said he would train me so that I could take the necessary exams. Of course, my real reason was that I hoped to get him back, but it hasn't worked.' She stopped again then said wryly, 'When I saw you and gradually realised that he was attracted to you I naturally became jealous.' She shrugged again. 'Well, I'm over that now. I've decided to go back to Shropshire, where I've got lots of friends.'

It was a long speech, but only one point stood out in Sophie's mind. She stared at Dawn disbelievingly.

'Robert isn't attracted to me. It's my practice he wants—you said as much yourself some time ago.'

'Oh, yes. He wants that, but he wants you, too. You go with the practice, so to speak.'

Sophie winced involuntarily, then she laughed scornfully.

'A nice thought,' she said, and tried to keep the bitterness out of her voice.

Dawn's eyes held a hint of mockery, but she said no more. Instead she got up and went to look at the Labrador. 'She's beginning to come round. What do you think?'

Sophie felt the dog's reflexes. 'So far, a normal recovery. I'll watch over her while you go back. You must have lots to do. Thank you for helping me. I couldn't have managed alone.' She smiled. 'It's nice to be on friendly terms. I shall be sorry now if you leave your job.'

Dawn lifted her shoulders. 'No point in staying. Robert will have to find another veterinary nurse.'

Alone in the surgery Sophie sat deep in thought, trying to solve the problems that loomed. The slight movements from the recovery cage brought her back to the present and she felt a great sense of relief as she watched the gradual return to consciousness of her patient.

Then a car drew up in the courtyard and at the same time the telephone rang. She was writing down a message when she heard someone come into the room and knew without turning that it was Robert. Replacing the receiver, and without waiting for him to speak, she said hastily, 'A bad whelping case — I'll have to go.'

'Don't worry. Give me the address and I'll see to it. But first I want to say how sorry I am that I had to send Dawn to you instead of coming myself as I promised. I hope she told you why. A difficult calving.' He paused. 'How did the op go? Has your confidence returned?'

She nodded. 'Thankfully, yes. And Dawn was very helpful. As for this whelping case — I've just had a thought. No need for you to go. The owners have no transport, but I know Helen will be glad to fetch it. I'll just give her a ring.'

She picked up the telephone, but he stopped her.

'Why bother Helen when I'm free? First of all, though, will you give me a coffee, please? I've come straight from the calving and I didn't even get a cup of tea when I'd finished. A very tight-fisted farmer.'

She glanced at him quickly and saw that he did

indeed look tired. Yet he was insisting on going to a whelping case. She flushed guiltily as she put on the kettle.

'It's kind of you to help when you've got your own practice to run. Are you very busy?'

'At the moment, yes, because Ian is spending a lot of time with Joanna. By the way, that girl's got some guts. She's coming out today, I gather. Ian said he was fetching her at lunchtime.' He smiled ruefully. 'I can see that eventually I shall lose my very good assistant and you will lose your partner. And before that happens I shall lose Dawn. Did she tell you that she's going back to Shropshire?'

'Yes.' Sophie spoke carefully. 'We had a long talk about the future.' She stopped, then added meaningly, 'And the past.'

'The past? Whose past?'

'Well, hers, of course, and yours as well.' She was pleased to see his embarrassment. She added smoothly, 'Not that that had anything to do with me, but I couldn't stop her. She was in a confiding mood.'

Robert gazed at her steadily. 'I'd like to know what she told you, but I don't suppose you'll tell me.'

'No. As I said, it's nothing to do with me.'

He finished his coffee. 'Well, I'd better go.' He picked up the address, read it, and thrust it into his pocket. Turning at the door, he said, 'Of course, if a Caesarean is necessary I'll bring it back to you.' He stopped, as though a sudden thought had struck him. 'It's beginning to work, isn't it?'

'What is?' Puzzled, Sophie rose to her feet and stared, waiting for his explanation.

'Why, the merging of our two practices. Ian and I are doing what any neighbouring colleagues would do

VETS IN OPPOSITION

in similar circumstances — and this helping-out is bearing fruit. It's all leading towards the inevitable — one good-sized mixed practice controlling a large area.' He must have seen the blaze of fury in Sophie's eyes, but, ignoring it, he added smilingly, 'Fate seems to have taken a hand in our affairs.'

She drew a long, angry breath. 'Well, fate has got it wrong — and so have you. You talk about the inevitable; as I see it, the inevitable is that you will have to move your mainly large-animal practice out into a more rural area, say, ten or twelve miles away. And even that wouldn't be far enough to please me.'

He laughed scornfully, but she saw that he had gone very pale. He said quietly, 'I don't think you mean what you're saying. I spoke of fate — surely if you listen to your heart, you will see that she has plans for us that go far beyond the merging of our two practices.'

He took a step towards her and, instinctively, Sophie drew back. Her voice trembled and her whole body stiffened as she stared at Robert incredulously.

'Plans? What plans?'

'I'll show you.'

Before she could escape she was in his arms and, for one sweet moment, she felt a flood of joy sweep through her. Then, like a dagger, Dawn's words stabbed into her brain and she struggled furiously as he bent to kiss her. She wrenched her head aside and gasped. 'Don't touch me. I hate your kisses and I hate you.'

He drew a sharp, hissing breath and released her abruptly, while tears of bitterness filled her eyes. He winced at the sight and drew back as though she had struck him.

'I'm sorry.' His voice was harsh and strained. 'I

thought you——God! I've made a terrible mistake. Please forgive me. I won't trouble you again.'

Then he was gone, and her tears fell like rain. Robert's sorrow and regret seemed genuine, but it all fitted in with what Dawn had told her. How could she love a man she didn't trust? Yet love him she did although she had told him she hated him. There was nothing she could do about it now, except try and force him out of her mind and heart. She poured herself a glass of water and, sipping it slowly, she began to recover. Above all, she must hide her feelings from Joanna and Helen. Their sympathy would be too much to bear and their advice would be impossible to follow. Her secret love for Robert must stay hidden, and perhaps eventually it would die a slow and painful death.

The arrival of Joanna, brought from hospital by Ian, distracted her from sorrowful thoughts, for which she was thankful. Sophie welcomed her warmly and pulled out a chair for the plastered leg to stretch out on, and soon they were joined by Helen. While they were drinking tea, Joanna regaled them with her story of her stay in hospital and made it all seem a huge joke. At last Helen said gently, 'You're getting tired. Let's go into the house. I'm sure you need a good rest.' She paused and smiled. 'I'm going to be your nurse. Sophie is managing very well, so there's nothing to worry about.'

Joanna sighed. 'Ian is going to do my farm work, such as it is, but I'll be sorry not to be able to attend to Mr Jarvis's pigs.'

Ian laughed. 'When you're a bit stronger, I'll drive you over there each time he calls me in,' he said, and Joanna looked at him so gratefully that tears burned at the back of Sophie's eyes. This was real love, love that was tender, caring and unselfish. How lucky they were.

Later that evening, when the Labrador had been handed over to its rejoicing owners, Sophie went into Joanna's room and found her looking pensive.

In answer to Sophie's question, she said, 'Ian says that when we're married he won't let me treat farm animals.'

'Oh, dear,' Sophie laughed, 'that's a bit dictatorial. Are you going to do everything he tells you to do? Surely that's not in your character?'

Joanna shrugged. 'I think characters change when love takes over. Mind you, I've gone off cows a bit. Pigs, though—that's different. They're my favourites, so I shan't give them up. I'll make it a condition before getting married.'

In bed that night Sophie recalled Joanna's words. Was it really the case that characters changed when love took charge? If so, then Robert certainly wasn't in love with her. He still wanted his own way. She definitely didn't come first with him. As Dawn had said, she, Sophie, went with the practice, and if he couldn't have the one than he wouldn't want the other.

CHAPTER TEN

FOR over a week Sophie heard no more from Robert. It was a busy time, for, with the arrival of autumn, the prospect of the dreaded kennel cough began to loom. For that, a preventative treatment had been produced. It was a live vaccine and provided immunisation for at least six months for healthy dogs. So far, there had been no outbreak in the district, but, acting on the principle that prevention was better than cure, many clients brought in their dogs to be vaccinated. This vaccination was no easy one to administer, for the necessary dose had to be given intra-nasally. A specially designed applicator was supplied, which minimised damage to local tissue. In the case of small dogs, half the dose had to be put into each nostril, and with large dogs the full dose was put into one nostril. When Sophie did these vaccinations in the pet shop Mr Miller held each patient so firmly and expertly that the recipient hardly noticed was was happening until it was over, but in the surgery it was sometimes traumatic. Often capable-looking owners assured her that they were good at controlling their pets, but at the first sign of resistance they released their hold and the animal then became nervous and upset. Finally Sophie had to stop her clients from giving their ineffectual help, and then Helen with her calm, soothing manner proved invaluable. It was not, however, a treatment that Sophie liked giving.

At the end of one particularly difficult morning

surgery, she sat down for coffee with a long sigh of relief.

'Thank goodness for that,' she said feelingly. 'I thought that tough little Jack Russell would finally get the better of me.'

Helen smiled. 'I suppose I'd better have my two dogs done to be on the safe side. I've only met kennel cough once and that was last year, when a dog belonging to a friend caught it after having been boarded out when she had to go away for a few weeks. The cough sounds ghastly — harsh and dry. It's quite alarming — though the dogs show no other signs of being upset. It's brought on by exercise and excitement.'

'It's a respiratory disease. But it can be helped by giving an injection and it will clear up of its own accord eventually. But it's very infectious, and you can't give the vaccine to pregnant bitches.'

Joanna came through from the dispensary to join them. She was walking now with a stick and as she sat down heavily at the table she seemed depressed. In answer to Sophie's enquiry, she shrugged.

'Nothing wrong. It's just that I'd like to be doing more outside work. I haven't seen much of Ian either — he's been pretty busy. Still —— ' she brightened up ' — he'll be coming round this evening. He told me on the phone that Dawn will be leaving in a fortnight's time and they haven't found a veterinary nurse to take her place. I shouldn't have thought it was all that difficult.'

'Neither would I,' Sophie said. 'There's always lots of advertisements in the *Veterinary Record* — fully trained nurses or girls wanting to be trained.'

'True, but Ian says the job they're offering isn't every girl's choice. They like to be in a large practice on the whole with other veterinary nurses. It's more interesting and more sociable. Goodness knows, it's not a job that's very lucrative, so they naturally want the best conditions.' She stopped. 'Listen — someone in the waiting-room. A late client, just as we're having coffee.'

But her frown turned into a smile as Mr Jarvis came in.

'How nice to see you,' she said. 'And how are the pigs?'

'Doing fine so far. I like that Mr Woodall — he's good, though I don't think he's got the feeling for pigs that you have.'

Invited to join them for coffee, he sat down, enquired after the progress of Joanna's bad leg, then relapsed into a rather uneasy silence.

Joanna looked at him thoughtfully. 'What's the trouble? Are you still worried about Blue Ear Disease?'

He looked up. 'That I am. I hear that there's still no vaccine for it.'

'That's true. But it hasn't come anywhere near us — it's mostly up north.' She paused. 'I've been reading about it in the *Veterinary Record* and I've cut out an article which deals with it. If you want to know its full name — ' she grinned ' — it's porcine reproductive and respiratory syndrome — otherwise PRRS. This article is quite informative.' She searched in her overall pocket. 'Here it is — three pages. They say — this was the result of a symposium of vets, including European ones — that it's a new disease that we'll have to live with for the forseeable future.'

Mr Jarvis groaned. 'As if life weren't difficult enough. It makes you wonder if pigs are worth it.'

'Of course they are,' Joanna said bracingly. 'You

know how you like them and how interesting they are. Now, in this article you'll find information to help prevent the disease as far as possible. I've underlined the important bits.'

'Ah, now that's just what I need.' Mr Jarvis looked more cheerful. 'Just so long as I can do something—no matter what—I won't feel so helpless.'

He took the paper eagerly and folded it carefully into his wallet. Then, as he drank the rest of his coffee, he said, 'Mr Woodall tells me that their veterinary nurse is going to leave.' He laughed. 'Can't say I'm sorry. Bit of a dragon, she is. He asked me if I knew of anyone to replace her and I told him no. Since then I've been thinking it over and I've come up with an idea. Don't know if she'd be what he and Mr Sheldrake want, but I've got a niece who's just leaving school. A nice, sensible girl, mad on animals, and very helpful to me at times. She always wanted to be a vet, but she's not up to the exams. I think she'd like to be a nurse, though.' He hesitated. 'I wondered if you'd mention it to Mr Woodall. I don't like to do it myself—it'd look as though I was pushing my niece forward.'

'Of course I'll tell him. A girl like that sounds ideal. I'll be seeing him tonight,' Joanna promised, and when he had gone she turned to Sophie. 'As I said, Ian's coming round this evening, but I'm a bit puzzled. He said he had some news, but it was only for my ears and I must keep it confidential. I can't think what it could be, can you?'

Sophie frowned. 'Can't imagine. You mustn't tell me—or Helen?'

'Apparently not.' Joanna paused then smiled mischievously. 'I haven't actually promised not to. I just said I couldn't wait to hear it. He won't get any promises from me.'

'Well, he won't tell you, then,' Helen said practically. 'If it's confidential, then you really must keep it to yourself.'

Joanna looked suitably rebuked. She shrugged ruefully. 'I suppose I'll have to. Still, it's probably not all that important. It may be something to do with Dawn leaving the practice, and I can't say that's terribly interesting.' She sighed as she prepared to get up. 'I'll be jolly glad when this plaster is off.'

'I think you manage remarkably well,' Helen said, 'and the fact that you do makes me wonder if I could hold my party after all. I put it off indefinitely because of your accident, but now Edward tells me he is going to America on business for ten days, and I'd like to have it before he goes next Monday. Would you mind coming in your present state, Joanna?'

'Of course not.' Joanna grinned. 'I love parties, and this leg won't stop me from enjoying myself.' She paused. 'Will you be inviting Ian?'

'Naturally, and Robert, too, if he'll come.'

Sophie swallowed hard. 'Would you mind very much if I didn't come?'

'I thought you'd say that,' Helen said calmly, 'and I would mind. Very much.' She shook her head slowly. 'Listen, Sophie. I know—we both know——' she glanced at Joanna '—that things are difficult between you and Robert. But you can't run away and hide as though you were afraid of him.'

Sophie flushed. 'I'm not running away. I just don't want to meet him socially. He makes me angry every time I see him, that's all.'

'Well, I shall be angry too if you don't come,' Helen

said sharply, then added more gently, 'I understand how you feel about him, but you ought to try and overcome your dislike. He's been very helpful to you since Joanna has been out of action.' She looked steadily at her goddaughter. 'Admit it—he has, hasn't he?'

Sophie shrugged. 'Yes, of course he has. But any neighbouring vet would have done the same.'

'Not necessarily,' Joanna put in. 'They might have helped out with the work, but Robert has done much more—lent you his nurse for that pyometra and lent Ian to do my farm work—and he's worked doubly hard himself. Why are you so ungrateful?'

It was hard for Sophie to face the kindly accusation in the two pairs of eyes gazing at her.

'You make me feel awful,' she said at last. 'The trouble is that I know that all the time he's only trying to ingratiate himself in order to get me to agree to a merger. Now wait a minute. . .' She saw them about to protest. 'It's true. Every time we meet he brings up the subject, and Dawn says—'

'Dawn says. . .' Joanna took her up sharply. 'Surely you don't go by what she says. You may have got quite friendly now, but she doesn't necessarily know all that goes on in Robert's mind.'

'Well, I do believe her,' Sophie said defiantly. 'He's very ambitious—would like to make our two practices into one large one that would control all this area and perhaps beyond. He told me so himself.'

'What's wrong with that?' Joanna demanded. 'It's what happens nowadays. It's the only way to survive. One vet on his or her own almost inevitably gets absorbed into a larger one, or fees must be kept so low that it isn't profitable.' She paused. 'In our case, it's a little different. Our small-animal practice is doing well and Robert's large-animal one likewise. That's how it's turned out, so why not carry it through—form one good mixed practice and later on expand still further?'

Sophie said nothing, though the answer was in her mind. It was because it meant abandoning her dream of a small country practice jogging happily along and not having anything to do with what she thought of as empire-building.

Surprisingly, Joanna seemed to read her thoughts.

'I think you're being old-fashioned. And not very realistic. There are so many disadvantages to a vet being on his or her own—on call for twenty-four hours, no time off, expensive locums for holidays, and everything depending on good health.'

'All right, all right. . .' Sophie said bitterly. 'You've made your point, but I heard all these objections at the veterinary congress. It didn't put me off then, and it doesn't now. The only difference is that I'm not a solo vet. I have a good partner—you. And that is a great advantage. When you leave, when you marry Ian, I shall try to go it alone, but if it is really too difficult then I'll get an assistant who, maybe, will become a partner. That's how I want it to be.'

There was a long silence until Helen spoke.

'Your plans are quite praiseworthy, Sophie, and I respect you for sticking to them. But it's still best to be on friendly terms with your neighbours, isn't it?' She waited till Sophie nodded reluctantly, then she added smoothly, 'So come to my party and don't make an enemy of the man who has proved to be such a good neighbour.'

There was nothing for Sophie to say after that and she resigned herself to the prospect of meeting Robert again, but later that morning, while she was working alone in the office, she felt desperately unhappy. All the things that Helen and Joanna had said were true, but Dawn's words cast a blight on the feelings of gratitude she ought to have.

The entry of Joanna, who came in to consult her about the drugs needed to replenish their stock, put an end to her melancholy reflections, and after they had decided Joanna said, 'When Ian comes round this evening I thought I'd give him coffee or a drink in our sitting-room. Will that be OK?'

Sophie laughed. 'I can take a hint. I won't interrupt you. I'll go up and stay with Helen.'

Joanna nodded absently. She said slowly, 'I can't help wondering what he has to tell me. It makes me a bit apprehensive. He sounded so mysterious.'

'Perhaps he wants you to marry him immediately.' Sophie smiled. 'Let's hope he doesn't want you to hobble up the aisle with a leg in plaster.'

'He should be so lucky.' Joanna grinned. 'Anyway, I've promised not to go until this practice is flourishing, and I'm sticking to that.'

'Well, you'll soon find out. But marrying Ian doesn't mean you have to leave here. You've got a long way to go before you can set up on your own. You could both stay on in your respective jobs. Besides, you don't know what he's going to tell you.' She shrugged her shoulders and laughed. 'He may have some dreadful secret in his past that he wants to confess to you—something that may shake you to the core.'

'Well, then...' Joanna suddenly giggled. 'What are you saying? Honestly, Sophie—don't you trust any man at all?'

Sophie flushed. 'Let's just say there's one man I

don't trust, but I'm not so bigoted that I'm a man-hater.' She hesitated. 'To tell you the truth, I really envy you and Ian. I just hope that one day I'll be as happy as you are.'

Later that day she recalled her own words and reflected wryly that the happy day would never arrive for her. But it was no use bemoaning her fate — she must make the best of it and hope that time would eventually heal the biggest wound she had ever experienced.

When that evening she made her way up to Helen's flat, she found that Edward was there. For one uncertain moment she thought they were in each other's arms, but as they welcomed her warmly, she decided that she had been mistaken. She apologised for being early, but Helen said, 'I was expecting you. We were talking about. . .' She stopped and glanced quickly at Edward. 'Shall I tell her?'

He nodded, smiling broadly. 'Yes. Why should we keep it a secret? Sophie — your darling godmother has consented to marry me.'

Sophie gasped with pleasure, but before she could say a word, Helen laughed.

'If you could see your face, Sophie. Do you think we're both mad? Too old for love?'

Drawing a long breath, Sophie shook her head and hugged her godmother so lovingly that Helen's eyes filled with tears. Then it was Edward's turn, and after that he said, 'I'm glad you approve, my dear. This calls for champagne. I've brought a bottle with me and put it in the fridge. Now where are the glasses?'

It was a happy evening, and when Sophie left she asked, 'May I tell Joanna?'

'Yes, of course.' Helen's face was glowing. 'And tell her that my party will become an engagement party.'

Ian had gone when Sophie went downstairs, and Joanna was sitting looking very pensive. She turned and greeted her friend, then continued sitting in thoughtful silence. This was so unusual that Sophie asked curiously, 'I know you can't tell me, but I hope Ian's news wasn't anything bad. You look very depressed.'

Joanna shook her head. 'You've got me wrong. I'm not depressed. I'm just fighting my conscience. I'm dying to tell you, but — well, I haven't exactly promised, but Ian says it could cause trouble if I did.'

'What on earth. . .?' Sophie looked almost as surprised as she had been at Helen's news. She said carefully, 'Honestly, Joanna, if Ian doesn't want you to tell anyone, then you mustn't. But listen — I've got some news, too.'

It was Joanna's turn to be astonished. 'Well, there you are,' she said jubilantly. 'I said right at the beginning that it would be a good thing if those two got together. Do you remember? You said I was being too romantic.'

'Well, you certainly seem able to scent romance anywhere. You're a real matchmaker.'

'Not as good as all that.' Suddenly Joanna looked serious. Then, after a moment's hesitation, she burst out, 'Look, Sophie — in spite of what Ian says, I've got to tell you. I think you ought to know. It's about — it's to do with Robert.'

'Well, then, I certainly don't want to know,' Sophie said sharply. 'I'm not interested in his affairs.'

She went quickly into the kitchen and set a tray for coffee. What did it matter if it stopped her from sleeping? She would be awake for most of the night anyway.

A few minutes later Sophie placed the tray on the low table beside Joanna and began to discuss the news of Helen's engagement, but Joanna showed very little interest. At last Sophie got up.

'I'm off to bed. What about you? Would you like any help?'

'No, thanks. I'm managing very well now.' Joanna pulled herself up in her chair. 'It's no use, Sophie. You've got to listen. I'm serious. It concerns the practice.'

On her way to the door, Sophie stopped. 'The practice? What. . .?' She stared at Joanna in alarm. What trouble was Robert cooking up? What mischief was he planning? She sat down abruptly in the nearest chair. 'Well, you'd better tell me, hadn't you?'

Joanna nodded. 'You'll have to revise your opinion of Robert. He's going to give up his practice and move away. He's going to set up somewhere else — a long way from here, Ian says. He's negotiating the sale of his house — selling it to a consultant surgeon at Seabourne General Hospital, so there'll be no more opposition for you.'

Sophie's heart seemed to stop. Trying hard to control herself, she asked, 'Why? For heaven's sake, why?'

Joanna was watching her closely. She said slowly, 'That's what I asked, and Ian said. . .' She stopped. 'Do you really want to know what he said?'

'Of course I do. I'm absolutely stunned.'

'I think "shattered" would be a better word, don't you? From my observance, you're not exactly overjoyed, although in view of all you've said about Robert you ought to be rejoicing. But you're not, are you, Sophie?'

She ignored the searching question. 'Well—go on. What did Ian say was the reason?'

'It was only an idea he had, based on the way Robert has been behaving for some time. Actually he pinpointed it to the day I came back from hospital. Apparently Robert went to see you that morning after that operation you did with Dawn to help you. Ian says from then on Robert has been a changed man—withdrawn and completely unapproachable. Obviously something must have happened between you that caused the change. We can only guess, but I'm sure you know the reason. You must at least have a good idea.'

'Why on earth should you think that?' Sophie stared. 'I'm absolutely astounded.'

Joanna looked disappointed. 'I was certain you would know. That's why I've told you.'

She sat pondering while Sophie tried to come to terms with Robert's seemingly incomprehensible plan. A memory of the day mentioned by Joanna stirred at the back of her mind, but, not daring to examine it, she waited for Joanna to say something. When she did, Sophie's subconscious uneasiness became even stronger.

'The only person who isn't surprised is Dawn. She maintains that she and she alone knows why Robert is chucking everything up.' Joanna frowned. 'I find that hard to believe. There's no love lost between those two, according to Ian. Well, there it is. Apparently the sale of the house is going through, with the prospect of exchanging contracts at the end of the month.'

'What about Ian? He'll be out of a job.'

Joanna shook her head. 'Not for long. Only until Robert gets established in his new practice, though when or where that will be we haven't the faintest idea. But Ian has another idea. He suggests we get married and do what Robert is doing—set up on our own. And there we disagree. I've said no, not yet. So he'll probably do locums for a while.'

'Oh, dear,' Sophie said inadequately, then sat silently for a long minute. Then, looking up, she said, 'I've had a thought. If Robert really is going, then what about Ian coming here as assistant? There'll be all the farm work that Robert is leaving behind, so we could probably afford to pay him, at a pinch. Later on— when you decide to go—I could get a new assistant.'

She was thinking quickly, trying to ignore the aching pain in her heart. Then, suddenly, just as Joanna was nodding a dubious assent, the full force of what she had been told hit her like a thunderbolt. She had told Robert that she hated him, told him to go away, to move to another area, and he had taken that literally. He had gone white, she remembered, had said he had made a terrible mistake. He had thought—what had he thought? The question hammered in her brain and her great desire was to be alone. She said, 'Joanna, I simply must go to bed. I'm dead beat. We'll talk about all this in the morning.'

The tears that were burning at the back of her eyes began to fall as soon as she entered her room, and, flinging herself on the bed, she gave way to helpless misery. After a long time, her fighting spirit gradually revived and she began to think constructively. Robert was sacrificing his practice, along with his great interest in the zoo, in order that she should have no opposition. Furthermore, he was keeping it a secret until the day he moved out. Of course, he had to tell Ian, and Ian had felt bound to tell Joanna. So now the secret was out. But what difference did it make. Nothing would stop Robert from carrying out his plans unless — unless what? Suddenly she knew the answer, even as she asked herself the question, and realised what she had to do.

She sat opposite him in his office with the door firmly closed. When she had telephoned Robert about breakfast-time, asking to see him about an important matter, he had seemed so astonished that the only place he had been able to suggest was here. At the time this had seemed appropriate, but now she was regretting the formal atmosphere. He was waiting for her to open the conversation, but his manner was so cold and distant that she found it difficult to begin. At last, seeing the impatient glint in his eyes, she drew a long breath and said, 'I've been thinking things over — thinking very deeply — and I've come to the conclusion that your idea of merging our two practices is, after all, the most sensible solution to our problem.' She paused and forced herself to look at him steadily, but his expression gave nothing away. Suddenly she felt at a loss. She had said it all and now it was his turn to speak. The silence seemed interminable, but at last he said curtly, 'Go on.'

It was humiliating, and she had not expected that kind of reaction from him. Determined not to be put down, she said, 'There's really no more to add except that I would like to know if you are still of the same opinion.'

He took up a pen and drew a few lines on a notepad — meaningless lines that irritated her as she watched. Suddenly he looked up and slowly shook his head.

'No. I've changed my mind. It's too late.'

Carefully trying to keep all emotion from her voice, in spite of a cold shock that went right through her, she asked, 'But you were the one who suggested it. Why have you abandoned the idea? You said it was the only reasonable thing to do, yet now, when at last I agree, you say it's too late.' She paused, drew a long breath, and said almost appealingly, 'I don't understand.'

Suddenly he passed his hand over his eyes as though he wanted to hide any emotion from her, and his mouth tightened into a grim line. His voice was strained and harsh.

'You never have understood. You thought my motives were suspect, that all I wanted was to get control of your practice and eventually edge you out altogether. You despised me for that and finally told me you hated me. Hardly a good basis for a successful partnership.' He paused and she saw that his face looked drawn and pale. He added slowly, 'Now I'm the one who fails to understand. Why do you come to me with a proposal for something you have resisted all along?'

She sought desperately for an answer, but could find none. This discussion was proving to be a disaster. She had not anticipated a flat refusal. What more could she say to prevent him from carrying out his plan to move out of the village?

He rephrased his question. 'Why this sudden change of mind? You don't need help with your practice — I gather the small-animal work is thriving.'

This was easier to answer. She said, 'Well, that's a good reason for merging, isn't it? Your practice — the farm work in particular—is also thriving, from what I hear. To form one good mixed practice would be to our mutual advantage. You said so yourself.'

'From the business point of view that's true. But what about the personal side? A partnership without trust? A partnership where one partner hates the other? How can you even consider such a scheme?' He shook his head slowly and decisively. 'As I said, it's too late. There's too much hostility between us.'

With as much dignity as she could muster Sophie stood up, and as he came from behind his desk to open the door she saw thankfully that there was no one in the surgery. She turned to say goodbye as she went outside, but, to her chagrin, he had returned to his office.

Outside in her car she kept a tight grip on herself, refusing to let her humiliation reduce her to tears. Instead of driving back to Broom House, she went into the village. Perhaps a strong black coffee would help her to face Helen and Joanna without betraying the shock of rejection she had suffered.

She sat in the little café in the High Street, then, having managed to calm herself enough to face the world, she prepared to leave. Bending down to pick up her bag, she jerked erect as a voice said, 'Sophie— what on earth are you doing here?'

Her heart sank as she saw Helen gazing at her in astonishment.

'I've just come to get some pastries for tea. . .' Helen stopped and gazed at her goddaughter searchingly. 'My dear! What's wrong? aren't you well?'

Sophie shook her head, but words failed her. She tried to smile, but without success, and Helen's concern grew. Pulling up a chair, she sat down. 'You've had a shock of some kind. Tell me — perhaps I can help. Wait — I'll just get a coffee and another one for you.'

She went to the counter and gave her order, then as she sat down again, she said, 'I mean it, Sophie. You've got to talk. Something is very wrong, and I can't bear to see you looking so sad.'

Her love and sympathy was too much for Sophie. She was so near to tears that her only outlet was to tell the whole sorry tale, including the news that Joanna had given her the day before. Then she poured out in detail the humiliation she had recently suffered, and at last she sighed deeply and said, 'You've caught me at my weakest, but I'm gradually pulling myself together.' She added slowly, 'I'll get over it eventually.'

Helen's face had gone pale and she sat in silence for a long minute. Then she said, 'I can scarcely believe that two young people so obviously in love with each other could be so utterly foolish.

Sophie's eyes widened and she sat bolt upright, staring incredulously at the calm figure sitting opposite.

'Utterly foolish,' Helen repeated, then she put out her hand and placed it over Sophie's. 'My dear, don't look so amazed. Do you think I'm blind? No need for you to deny it — no need to speak. If you want to know how I, and, incidentally, Joanna, are so sure that you and Robert love each other. . .well, it's in your eyes when you talk to him, in the way he tenses up when he sees you — there's a magnetism between you that is almost visible.' She laughed gently. 'Enough of that. You have a problem. Do you want my advice?'

Sophie nodded mutely and Helen smiled and patted her hand. 'Well, then, this is what you must do. Write to him immediately. Don't shake your head like that. You must put aside your pride. You owe him an apology for misjudging him and suspecting his motives at every turn. Then you must tell him that you most certainly do not hate him, that you were angry and spoke wildly when you said that. Tell him you would like to be friends, good friends.' She paused. 'Leave it at that. The rest is up to him. If you don't do that, Sophie, you will lose him forever. He's that kind of man.'

'But he doesn't love me—he's never mentioned love,' Sophie said dully, and Helen smiled.

'Never mind that. You will be just offering friendship. If he wants more he'll soon let you know.' She waited for a moment. 'Now are you going to write that letter or not?'

Sophie hesitated and swallowed hard. Then, almost hypnotised by her godmother's steady gaze, she said, 'Yes. Yes, I think I must. It can't make matters worse, anyway. Thank you for your advice.'

On her way back to the surgery, Sophie glanced at her watch and realised with a start that she had left Joanna on her own for nearly two hours. As she went in, she said apologetically, 'I'm so sorry, Joanna. I had an appointment—well, I'll explain later. How have you got on?'

'I managed.' Joanna grinned. 'One or two people came in, but nothing I couldn't cope with. By the way, Ian rang and wants to take me out tonight. Is that OK with you?'

'Of course.' Sophie nodded. 'You need a bit of life.'

'So do you.' Joanna paused. 'Well, you'll get some on Saturday. Remember? Helen's party.'

'The day after tomorrow... Goodness, I'd completely forgotten.' Sophie smiled mechanically, but her spirits sank. She must write that letter in time for him to send back a reply. She could never face him at the party if she didn't know where she stood—didn't know whether or not he had rejected her apology or was prepared to be friendly.

Using the excuse of some paper work, she settled down in the office and after following Helen's advice implicitly, she put the letter into an envelope, addressing it 'Personal'. Then a problem arose. How to deliver it? If she put it into his letter-box herself she might well be seen. She frowned anxiously, then suddenly her face brightened. Going upstairs to Helen's flat, she handed it over, and her godmother took it with a smile.

'I'll go and put it in his letter-box right away. Let's hope he'll deliver his reply the same way.'

Next morning Sophie searched through her post anxiously and was beginning to despair when, at the bottom of the pile, she found an unstamped envelope marked 'personal' and underlined. She opened it with a trembling hand and sat staring at it for a long time. It was brief and to the point, but it gave nothing away.

> Thank you for your letter. I look forward to seeing you at the party tonight.

A short time later, she showed it to Helen, who said calmly,

'Very nice.' Then meeting Sophie's anxious gaze, she said briskly, 'Now don't look so doubtful. Everything will turn out all right.'

Sophie frowned. 'I'm not so sure. I almost dread meeting him.'

'Don't be so feeble, Sophie. You sound like a Victorian miss. We're in the 1990s, not the 1890s.'

Her godmother's astringent words had their effect and suddenly Sophie's nervousness disappeared. She had done the right thing and Robert's note promised friendliness. That was all she had asked, and she would be content with that.

That evening she dressed with care. Her royal blue silk dress came out once more, her lustrous dark hair flowing on to her shoulders, and her beautiful eyes filled with joyful anticipation as she strolled into Joanna's room.

'You look fantastic!' Her friend's eyes opened wide. 'What have you been doing to yourself?'

Sophie laughed. 'Nothing special. Same dress. Same make-up.'

'All the same, you're all — what's the word? — aglow. I think it must be love. OK. OK. Don't look so fierce. I'm only joking.'

Joanna said no more, for which Sophie was thankful. She felt as though she were treading on thin ice and any false move might plunge her once more into the dark depths of despair.

Soft music filled Helen's rooms, and she and Edward looked so happy that Sophie rejoiced for them. Glancing carefully round at the little groups of guests she saw that Ian had already claimed Joanna, but there was no sign of Robert. For a moment her heart sank. Had he decided not to come after all or was he out on an urgent case? Then suddenly she saw him, and, as always, her heart jumped. She tried to look uninterested as she watched him go up to Helen and Edward, but when, after a minute or two, he turned and walked purposefully towards her, she knew a moment of near-panic.

Without preamble, he said, 'Helen says we can talk in that little room through there, where we won't be disturbed.' He took her arm and for a moment Sophie resented his high-handed manner. Then she met his eyes as he smiled down at her, and she knew instinctively that all would be well.

The room was small and very quiet and Sophie did nothing to break the silence. She sat down in an armchair, but Robert remained standing. At last he said, 'Your letter told me that you didn't mean it when you said you hated me. That, to me, was the most important point. You asked to be friends, and, of course, I agree, though really I want much more than that.' He stopped as he heard her gasp, then went on steadily, 'But I have a question to which I'd like to know the answer. What made you change your mind about merging our practices?'

She flushed, unwilling to betray Joanna and Ian. She said slowly and carefully, 'Well, you know how quickly gossip travels round here. I heard the other day that you were thinking of selling your practice and moving away.'

'Ah.' His eyes hardened. 'So you thought I would sell to another vet and that might make things worse for you on the principle that the devil you know is better than the devil you don't know.'

She said desperately, '*No*. It wasn't like that at all. I also heard that you were selling to a surgeon from the hospital.'

His eyebrows rose. 'Now only Ian knew that, so how. . .?' He shrugged and smiled grimly. 'I can guess. It wasn't just gossip, was it? Ian told Joanna, who then told you.'

'Well—oh, what does it matter? The fact is that I didn't—don't want you to make such a sacrifice and give up the zoo work you like so much.'

'Why should you care?' The harsh question made

her flinch, but she retorted, 'Why should you make such a sacrifice?'

He looked at her long and steadily. 'I realised that you definitely didn't want to merge and I would have accepted that, but when you said you hated me —' he paused '—well, that hit me hard. I decided then to get right out of your life.'

She stared at him speechlessly, hardly daring to believe the hidden meaning behind his words, then, just as she managed to find her voice, there was a knock at the door. Startled, she turned as Robert called, 'Come in,' and Joanna entered.

She said apologetically, 'I'm awfully sorry to interrupt, but if you remember, Sophie, we put the telephone through to Helen. Now a message has come in, about that pyometra you did. The bitch has collapsed. It sounds like a heart attack, and the owners are terribly worried. They want you right away. I had to tell you, but, if you like, either I or Ian will go for you.'

Already Sophie was on her feet and shaking her head, so Joanna continued, 'I've got the directions. It's a cottage about four miles from here. Are you sure you won't let either of us go?'

'Oh, no. Thank you very much, but this is my patient and I must see the case through. I'll go right away.'

'And I'll go with you,' Robert said firmly. 'Will you make my excuses to Helen, please, Joanna?'

She nodded and disappeared, but Sophie stood for a moment. 'There's no need for you to come,' she said. 'I can manage on my own.'

'Nevertheless, I'm coming,' he said smoothly. 'Now go and get your case and grab an overall. You mustn't spoil that beautiful dress.'

Once more she began to resent his authoritative manner, and he seemed to read her thoughts.

'I know,' he said drily. 'You don't like being bossed. Well, we haven't time to fight it out, so you may as well accept my company. What's more, I'll take you in my car.'

She shrugged ruefully, and ten minutes later they were speeding out of the village.

CHAPTER ELEVEN

SOPHIE and Robert were nearing Seabourne when, following Sophie's directions, Robert turned into a quiet lane and stopped outside a pretty cottage. Before they could get out of the car, Sophie's client came down the path to open the gate.

'Mr Hobden, this is Robert Sheldrake, who has been good enough to come with me, so you'll have the benefit of two opinions.' Sophie saw him look anxiously at an upper window as he acknowledged the introduction, then he said 'We have to speak very quietly as our little girl is asleep and she doesn't know that Sandy is ill.'

Sophie nodded understandingly and Robert shut the car doors very carefully. Then they followed Mr Hobden into the house. In the sitting-room Mrs Hobden rose to her feet and indicated a large dog basket.

'She's sleeping now, but we thought she was going to die in that last attack.'

Sophie bent down to examine her patient. Her breathing was laboured and she was now in a coma. Opening her case, she took out a syringe and filled it with a heart and respiratory stimulant. As soon as she had given the injection she massaged the area briskly to help the dispersal of the drug. Then, from, her case, she took out a bottle of tablets.

'I think she'll come round in ten to fifteen minutes and I'd like to wait and make sure,' she said. 'Then these tablets should help to keep her going.'

Mrs Hobden went into the kitchen, and a few minutes later she came through the doorway carrying a tray. Robert jumped to his feet, but she waved him aside and placed the tea and biscuits on a nearby table.

'Something to keep us going,' she said, and managed a tearful smile. 'I reckon, though, that James and I would probably do better with a dose of that injection you've just given Sandy.'

They were a courageous couple and did their best to lighten the strained atmosphere as they all waited for the heart stimulant to work.

With her eyes fixed on the dog Sophie said suddenly, 'She's coming round.'

A few minutes later Sandy opened her eyes and turned her head slowly towards them. Mrs Hobden went down on her knees and stroked her gently, and as Sandy's tail wagged feebly at her touch she burst into tears.

'Try not to upset yourself too much,' Sophie said gently. 'Sandy will sense your distress.' Handing over the tablets, she gave the necessary instructions and added, 'That's all I can do, I'm afraid. I'll just sound her heart again before we go.'

Listening carefully, she frowned, and, putting aside her stethoscope, she turned to Robert and mutely invited him to give his opinion. He took the instrument and listened to Sandy's heart for what seemed a long time. Then he, too, frowned and was beginning to say something when suddenly there was one sharp whimper and, although Sophie did her best, Sandy was dead in a few minutes.

She rose from her knees to face two pairs of eyes in which hope had died at last. True to type, they took it well. Mrs Hobden wept — not so much, she explained, for the dog as for her daughter, who would suffer the most. Then she dried her eyes and offered more tea. Robert, who had been very silent, said suddenly, 'I know it's too soon, but your little daughter might feel her loss less deeply if you gave her another dog. Not quite a puppy, but one, say about six months old.'

The parents glanced at each other and Mrs Hobden nodded slowly.

'I've been thinking the same thing. But we don't know how to set about it. I know it will be a bit expensive, but Chrissie comes first in our lives.'

'Well, I know just the dog—bitch, I should say. Six months old, spayed—I did the operation myself—and in need of a loving home. Her owner would, I'm sure let her go for such a good cause. She's a black Labrador, gentle and docile, and, by the way, there would be no question of payment.'

They left the cottage, leaving a grateful if sad couple who were quite amazed at the way in which their problem had been solved. So, indeed, was Sophie, and as soon as they were in the car she asked, 'Is your story true? Do you really know of a Labrador like that or are you——'

'True?' he interrupted fiercely. 'Of course, it's true. Really, Sophie, don't you trust me in any way at all? Do you think I was making it all up just to console the Hobdens?'

'No, of course not. But "no question of payment"—that's hard to believe.'

'The bitch is mine,' he said shortly. 'I've just taken her over from a friend who is going abroad. She's only been with me a week, and I think that a handicapped child's need is greater than mine.'

Suddenly Sophie caught her breath on a sob and her

eyes filled with tears. He shot her a quick glance and pulled into the side of the road.

His arm went round her shoulder and he said, 'Please don't cry. I know it's upsetting to lose a patient, but — '

'It's not that.' She stopped. She couldn't tell him how his generosity had moved her, couldn't tell him how she had misjudged him all along. She felt for a tissue to wipe tears that were falling uncontrollably, and, seeing her need, he took a large handkerchief from his pocket and, turning her face to his, he very gently wiped her eyes.

In the darkness of the car, she felt instinctively that he was about to kiss her, then to her dismay he seemed to change his mind. Instead he took his arm away and asked, 'Better now?'

She nodded, disappointed that he was being so matter-of-fact, and, pulling herself together, she stared out of the window as the headlights shone on the hedges and fields of the countryside they were passing through. Suddenly she said, 'You've missed the Wakefield turning. You're going to Seabourne.'

'I know,' he said tersely, then, slowing down, he asked, 'Which would you rather do — go back to the party or drive up on to the Downs overlooking the sea and take a little stroll?'

His meaning was clear, and she knew the choice before her was a momentous one, one that might change the whole course of her life.

She said calmly, 'Let's go up on the Downs. It's a beautiful night.'

It was indeed. There was no moon, but a sky sparkling with brilliant stars, and as she got out of the car the sweet, sharp air almost took her breath away.

He took her hand as they walked slowly along the cliff edge, and a feeling of peace and security swept over her. This was a man she could trust and this was the man she loved. He was a strong man, yet full of compassion and tenderness. He said he wanted much more than just friendship, and so did she. Nevertheless, friendship was important, and that they now had in full. The next step must be taken by him—she was content to wait and revel in the certainty that he would, eventually, tell her that he loved her.

That moment came unexpectedly. Looking down at the reflection of the stars in the still, calm sea below, she said softly, 'I'm glad we came up here. It's so beautiful, isn't it?'

He said quietly, 'Not as beautiful as you are,' and suddenly he swept her into his arms. For a second, she was so startled that she automatically stiffened, and he drew back.

'Sophie—I love you.' His voice was strained. 'You must know that by now, but do you love me?'

The words were what she had longed to hear, and she stayed silent, savouring the most wonderful moment of her life. Then he said urgently, 'Please— please, Sophie, don't torture me. Do you love me?'

She came to life, put her arms round his neck, and stroked his hair.

'I think I've loved you from the first moment I saw you,' she said, and drew in her breath sharply as he crushed her against him. As their lips met, she knew in a flash that this kiss of love was even more wonderful than the words that had just thrilled her. Yielding to his caresses, she revelled in the fact the he found her desirable. At last he drew back, and his voice was almost stern.

'My darling, I want you so much. It's sheer torture to hold back, but I must. I know how you feel about it. . . You would rather wait—wait till we're married. Am I right?'

She hesitated. Her whole being was aflame with desire for him, but the question that he asked was so tender, so loving, that she knew the answer she gave would be the one that he subconsciously wanted to hear. She said softly, 'I want you, too, but. . .' she stopped, but it was enough.

Burying his face in her hair, he murmured something, then he lifted his head and said, 'It will be a wonderful wedding night, my love.'

He showered her with kisses, and time seemed to stand still for them both, until at last he said reluctantly, 'It's no use. I must take you back or my resolution will break down.'

It was then that she realised her own power and made an instant resolve never to abuse it. As they walked back to the car, he took her hand again and then lifted it to his lips. He said very quietly, 'I'll never let you down, my darling. I'm yours forever.'

Driving back, there was no more need for words. Occasionally, he took his hand off the gear lever and reached out for hers, and sometimes he glanced towards her with a look so full of tenderness that she felt she could weep for joy.

The party was over and the house was in darkness when he pulled up in the courtyard and accompanied her through the front door into the hall. It was then, with opportunity beckoning, that their mutual resolve wavered. Then, in a voice that was almost stern, he said, 'When I look in your eyes I'm absolutely lost. But

I really must leave you. Sophie, darling, we must get married as soon as possible.'

She laughed gently. 'As soon as it can be arranged. Helen will want the wedding to take place from here, but I'll have to hold her back from making it into such a big affair that it will take months to prepare.'

'Months? My God!' He held her close. 'I can't wait that long.'

She shook her head. 'Weeks rather than months,' she promised. 'I'll see to that.' She lifted her face to his, then jumped suddenly as the telephone sounded.

'A night call,' he said. 'How damnable.' And he waited as she picked up the receiver.

'An accident? Where?' She paused. 'Can't you get anyone nearer? Oh, very well. I'll be along as soon as possible.'

Replacing the instrument, she turned to Robert.

'A dog — run over — badly hurt. It's on the road to Westmead. We're the only vets they've been able to contact.' She sighed. 'It's a bit much, isn't it?' She turned away. 'I must get my case.'

He drew her back. 'If you think I'm going to let you turn out at this time of night you've got another think coming. This is where our practices merge. In future, I'll do all the night calls.' He held her tight for a moment, then released her reluctantly. Then as he went towards his car she stiffened suddenly. 'Just a minute, Robert. Come back to being a vet. I don't like the sound of your last statement.'

His eyebrows rose and he met her steady gaze with a hint of amusement in his own.

'No need to get your hackles up. What have I said to annoy you?'

She drew a long breath. 'It's your dictatorial attitude.

You say that, in future, you will do all night calls. What other rules are you going to make? Are you going to take over patients that you consider too difficult for me? Are you going to dispute the fees I charge? And what about——' She stopped as the telephone rang again. Reluctantly she picked it up and listened for a moment.

'Are you absolutely sure? Soon after you rang me. . . Well, I certainly couldn't have got there in time. Thank you for telling me.' She replaced the instrument and turned back to Robert. 'The dog is dead.'

He shrugged. 'Well, that's that. Now you can continue your attack on me.'

She swallowed hard. 'It's not an attack. It's a request for information. I want to know if, as partners, we shall be equal in every way. Absolutely equal. No decisions taken without mutual agreement.' She paused. 'And, later on, will you be a domineering husband and try to turn me into a docile, obedient wife?' She stopped as he began to shake with suppressed laughter, then added indignantly, 'I'm serious, Robert. Please answer my questions.'

With obvious difficulty he controlled his mirth, but his voice was choked as he said, 'You? A docile, obedient wife? That is beyond imagination!' Then, suddenly, his expression changed and he frowned. 'Sophie—I don't like that word "domineering". Do you honestly think that's what I'll be?' The colour drained from his face. 'My darling—I love you. . . adore you. . .respect you. . .' His voice broke and for a moment he stood silent, then, very quietly, he added, 'You will always be my guiding star.'

A lump rose in Sophie's throat. She reached out to him and he took her gently into his arms. As she looked up at him she saw such tenderness, such deep love in his eyes that her own filled with tears. They stood clasped together for a long time, then he bent his head and kissed her, softly at first, then with such increasing passion that she could feel his heart beating like a drum. At last he lifted his head.

'As regards the practice — '

'Oh, no! Not that any more.' She felt light-headed, almost faint with love. 'I know it will be all right. I trust you and you can trust me. We'll work it out together.' She paused, then smiled mischievously. 'One thing I'll allow you...if we really can't agree on something—say, like going out on night calls—then you shall decide.'

He considered this thoughtfully, then a gleam of amusement came into his eyes. 'As to that, I think once we're married we'll get an assistant vet who is a bachelor. Then he can do the night calls and our connubial bliss won't be interrupted.'

Later, after watching him drive away, Sophie turned back into the house. It was then that she saw a soft glow of light in Helen's bedroom.

For a moment she hesitated. Should she go up and tell her godmother all that had happened? She stood still, pondering, then slowly she shook her head. It was too soon. She needed to keep it all to herself for a few hours — hours in which she could live that precious time over and over again, recall his kisses, his voice and, above all, the look in his eyes. A look that claimed her for his own and spoke of a love that would bind them together for always.

MILLS & BOON

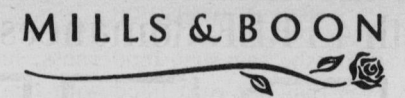

CHRISTMAS KISSES...

...THE GIFT OF LOVE

Four exciting new Romances to melt your heart this Christmas from some of our most popular authors.

ROMANTIC NOTIONS — Roz Denny
TAHITIAN WEDDING — Angela Devine
UNGOVERNED PASSION — Sarah Holland
IN THE MARKET — Day Leclaire

Available November 1993   *Special Price only £6.99*

*Available from W. H. Smith, John Menzies, Martins, Forbuoys, most supermarkets and other paperback stockists.
Also available from Mills & Boon Reader Service, FREEPOST, PO Box 236, Thornton Road, Croydon, Surrey CR9 9EL. (UK Postage & Packing free)*

Discover the thrill of *Love on Call* with 4 FREE Romances

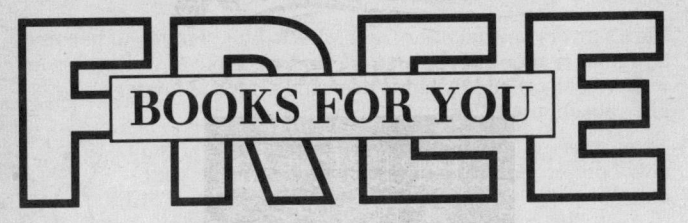

FREE
BOOKS FOR YOU

In the exciting world of modern medicine, the emotions of true love acquire an added poignancy. Now you can experience these gripping stories of passion and pain, heartbreak and happiness - with Mills & Boon absolutely FREE! AND look forward to a regular supply of *Love on Call* delivered direct to your door.

🌹 🌹 🌹

Turn the page for details of how to claim 4 FREE books AND 2 FREE gifts!

An irresistible offer from Mills & Boon

Here's a very special offer from Mills & Boon for you to become a regular reader of *Love on Call*. And we'd like to welcome you with 4 books, a cuddly teddy bear and a special mystery gift - absolutely FREE and without obligation!

Then, every month look forward to receiving 4 brand new *Love on Call* romances delivered direct to your door for only £1.80 each. Postage and packing is FREE! Plus a FREE Newsletter featuring authors, competitions, special offers and lots more...

This invitation comes with no strings attached. You may cancel or suspend your subscription at any time and still keep your FREE books and gifts.

It's so easy. Send no money now but simply complete the coupon below and return it today to:

Mills & Boon Reader Service, FREEPOST, PO Box 236, Croydon, Surrey CR9 9EL.

--- NO STAMP NEEDED ---

YES! Please rush me 4 FREE *Love on Call* books and 2 FREE gifts! Please also reserve me a Reader Service subscription. If I decide to subscribe, I can look forward to receiving 4 brand new *Love on Call* books for only £7.20 every month - postage and packing FREE. If I choose not to subscribe, I shall write to you within 10 days and still keep the FREE books and gifts. I may cancel or suspend my subscription at any time simply be writing to you.
I am over 18 years of age.   Please write in BLOCK CAPITALS

Ms/Mrs/Miss/Mr _____   EP62D

Address _____

_____

_____ Postcode _____

Signature _____

Offer closes 31st March 1994. The right is reserved to refuse an application and change the terms of this offer. One application per household. Offer not valid to current Love on Call subscribers. Offer valid only in UK and Eire. Overseas readers please write for details. Southern Africa write to IBS, Private Bag, X3010, Randburg, 2125, South Africa. You may be mailed with offers from other reputable companies as a result of this application. Please tick box if you would prefer not to receive such offers. ☐

mps MAILING PREFERENCE SERVICE

ESCAPE INTO ANOTHER WORLD...

...With Temptation Dreamscape Romances

Two worlds collide in 3 very special Temptation titles, guaranteed to sweep you to the very edge of reality.

The timeless mysteries of reincarnation, telepathy and earthbound spirits clash with the modern lives and passions of ordinary men and women.

Available November 1993   Price £5.55

MILLS & BOON

Available from W. H. Smith, John Menzies, Martins, Forbuoys, most supermarkets and other paperback stockists.
Also available from Mills & Boon Reader Service, FREEPOST, PO Box 236, Thornton Road, Croydon, Surrey CR9 9EL. (UK Postage & Packing free)

MILLS & BOON

LOVE ON CALL

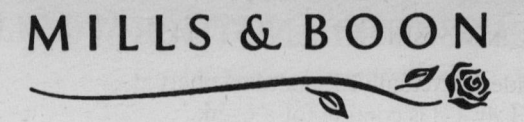

The books for enjoyment this month are:

SWEET DECEIVER Jenny Ashe
VETS IN OPPOSITION Mary Bowring
CROSSMATCHED Elizabeth Fulton
OUTBACK DOCTOR Elisabeth Scott

♥ ♥ ♥ ♥ ♥

Treats in store!

Watch next month for the following absorbing stories:

SECOND THOUGHTS Caroline Anderson
CHRISTMAS IS FOREVER Margaret O'Neill
CURE FOR HEARTACHE Patricia Robertson
CELEBRITY VET Carol Wood

Available from W.H. Smith, John Menzies, Volume 1, Forbuoys, Martins, Tesco, Asda, Safeway and other paperback stockists.

Also available from Mills & Boon Reader Service, Freepost, P.O. Box 236, Croydon, Surrey CR9 9EL.

Readers in South Africa - write to:
Book Services International Ltd, P.O. Box 41654, Craighall, Transvaal 2024.